TRACK OF THE ZOMBIE

THE HARDY BOYS ® MYSTERY STORIES

TRACK OF THE ZOMBIE

Franklin W. Dixon

Illustrated by Leslie Morrill

WANDERER BOOKS
Published by Simon & Schuster, New York

Manufactured in the United States of America
10 9 8 7 6 5 4 3 2 1

THE HARDY BOYS is a trademark of Stratemeyer Syndicate,
registered in the United States Patent and Trademark Office

WANDERER and colophon are trademarks of Simon & Schuster

Library of Congress Cataloging in Publication Data
Dixon, Franklin W.
Track of the zombie.
(The Hardy boys mystery stories ; 71)
Summary: The Hardy boys travel to Vermont to
investigate a mysterious fire and to help a circus
owner who is plagued with accidents.
[1. Mystery and detective stories. 2. Circus—
Fiction. 3. Vermont—Fiction] I. Morrill, Leslie H., ill.
II. Title. III. Series: Dixon, Franklin W.
Hardy boys mystery stories ; 71.
PZ7.D644Tr   [Fic]   81–16132
ISBN 0–671–42348–7   AACR2
ISBN 0–671–42349–5 (pbk.)

Contents

1 A Strange Suspect

"Frank," Joe Hardy said to his brother, "what's that guy ahead of us up to?"

The boys were driving toward their home after taking part in a ball game at Bayport High stadium. Joe's comment referred to a green station wagon careening wildly out of a side road. It made a big circle, and then roared up the main street ahead of the Hardys.

Just then, a second car zoomed out of the side road, forcing Frank to brake suddenly to avoid a collision. It was a blue sedan, and it sped up the main street, too.

"A couple of speed demons," Joe complained. "They're way over the limit! Lucky you hit the brake in time, Frank. That sedan would have barreled right into us!"

"It's trying to force the station wagon off the road!" Frank cried out.

The two cars were now racing alongside each other. The right fender of the sedan was only inches away from the station wagon. Suddenly, there was the crunch of metal against metal, and the station wagon hurtled off the road into a ditch! It jolted to a stop in a cloud of dust, while the other car sped off.

Frank slowed down. "Joe, see if the driver of that wagon is all right. I'll go after the other guy."

Joe leaped from their yellow sports car before it stopped. Frank picked up speed again, and rapidly closed the gap between himself and the blue sedan. Both cars hurtled toward the railroad tracks. A locomotive, pulling a long line of freight cars, pounded toward the crossing.

The driver in front of Frank raced for the intersection at full speed. He peered back over his shoulder, and the boy caught a glimpse of a ghostly white face! Then the sedan shot across the tracks, barely clearing them as the locomotive thundered past its rear fender!

Forced to stop for the freight train, Frank realized that by the time it got past, there would be no point in resuming the chase. He'll be long gone, the boy

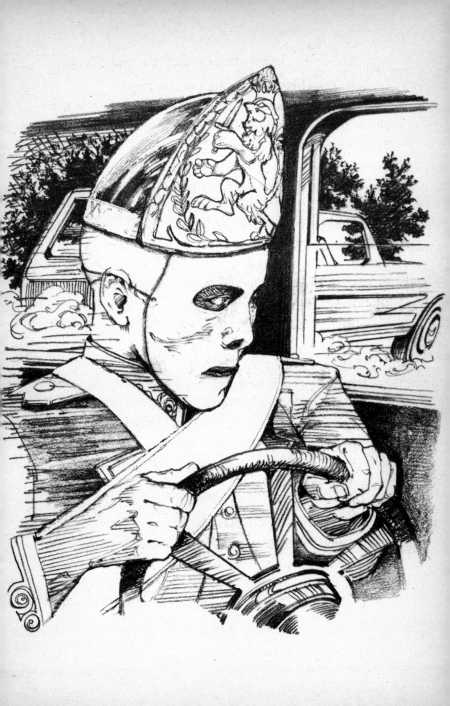

thought to himself, turning around and heading back in the direction he had come from.

He found Joe at the side of the road with a youth about their own age, who had a cut on his forehead. "His name's Rolf Allen," Joe revealed. "He isn't making much sense because he hit his head when the car stopped. He's very dizzy. We'd better take him to the hospital."

The Hardys helped Rolf into their car. Frank drove him to the medical center, with Joe following in Rolf's station wagon.

X-rays revealed no fracture, and the boy was released in the Hardys' care.

"Hey, thanks, guys, for helping me," he said. "And now I'd better be going."

"Where are you headed?" Joe asked.

"Bayport. Can't be too far from here."

"It sure isn't. You're *in* Bayport!"

"No kidding! With this guy on my tail, I just took the next exit on the highway without even realizing where I was."

"What do you want in Bayport?" Frank questioned.

"I'm looking for the Hardy boys."

The young detectives gasped. "We're Frank and Joe Hardy!" Frank exclaimed. "This is Joe, and I'm Frank."

"I'm in luck!" the boy cried out with a wide grin

on his face. "I came all the way from Vermont to see you!"

"Then I suggest we go home for dinner," Joe said. "You can tell us about yourself later."

Rolf gladly accepted the invitation, and the trio arrived at Elm Street as darkness was falling. They parked the cars in the driveway and the Hardys led their guest inside.

Mrs. Hardy was surprised to see Rolf, and quickly served a delicious meal of Irish stew with salad. Aunt Gertrude, Mr. Hardy's sister who had been living with the family for quite some time, stared questioningly at the young people.

"Now," she began with a severe expression, "what is going on here? I'll bet you're mixed up in another mystery!"

Frank and Joe grinned at each other. They were used to the tart comments of their aunt, who really was very fond of them and admired their skill as detectives. They quickly described how they had met Rolf, then asked their guest why he wanted to see them.

"I came to ask you to solve a mystery for me," Rolf explained. "I heard from my uncle, Mr. Bertrand of South American Antiquities, how you helped him in the mystery of *The Stone Idol*. I was on my way to this house when that other driver came after me. I tried to escape, but he was too fast.

11

I'm glad you were there to help me," Rolf conclud-ed gratefully.

"That was a real weirdo chasing you," Frank said. "His face gave me the creeps. It was completely white. Is he involved in your mystery?"

The youth from Burlington nodded. "He's the suspect!"

"Then you know him?"

Rolf twisted the button on his jacket nervously. "I know *about* him, Frank. This is the first time I ever saw him. And I just got a glimpse of his face. Completely white, as you said."

"Tell us everything from the beginning," Joe suggested.

"Okay. I'm from Hunter's Hollow, about twenty miles from Burlington, in the Green Mountains."

"Where Ethan Allen, the leader of the Green Mountain Boys, captured Fort Ticonderoga during the Revolution," Joe put in. "We've read about it. Terrific how they grabbed those cannons and hus-tled them over the mountains to Washington at Boston!"

"Ethan Allen is a relative of mine from way back," Rolf said. "And Fort Ticonderoga isn't far from where I live. Maybe the Green Mountain Boys came through Hunter's Hollow. My parents own a big house in the Hollow, all by itself in the woods. I was living there until they went on a European tour for several months. So was my friend, Lonnie Mindo."

"You mean, you moved out when your parents left on their trip?" Joe asked.

"Yes. Lonnie and I are taking acting classes at a studio in Burlington and he suggested that we move to a boardinghouse in town. Our schedule is so heavy with rehearsals and all, that we'd be going crazy if we had to commute. Also, my parents thought we'd be too lonely all by ourselves in that big old house."

Joe scratched his head. "But what's the mystery, Rolf?"

Rolf looked somber. "There was a forest fire near the house. It burned an acre of trees in the back. The underbrush is completely singed, and all you see are charred tree stumps. It took the whole Burlington Fire Department to put the fire out. The firemen think it may have been started by lightning or by someone carelessly dropping a match."

"Yes?" Frank prodded when Rolf paused.

"Well, I suspect it's arson! Somebody set the fire deliberately," the boy went on.

Frank was puzzled. "What could anyone gain from setting fire to the woods near your home?"

"Someone is trying to force my parents to sell the house, but they refuse to give it up. Before they left for Europe, they even rejected a hefty offer from a syndicate represented by a Burlington lawyer named Tyrell Tyson. For all I know, the same person is behind all of it."

Frank looked doubtful. "It doesn't seem likely that those people would send an arsonist to set the forest fire. They made an open bid for the house. Nothing sneaky about that."

"Oh, I don't really suspect the syndicate," Rolf declared. "But some mysterious person perhaps has his eye on the house and may be trying to get it any way he can. Look, just before Lonnie and I moved our things to the boardinghouse in Burlington, the phone rang. I answered it while Lonnie was stashing our suitcases in the car. A strange voice said the house would be burned if the Allens didn't sell pronto."

"Did you recognize the voice?" Joe queried. "Was it anyone you know?"

Rolf shrugged his shoulders in a gesture of hopelessness. "I had no way of telling. The voice was odd—squeaky, as if the guy were pinching his nose while he was talking into the telephone."

"But you think it was a man?" Joe asked.

"Yes, it probably was."

"Did he say anything else?" Frank wondered.

"He sure did," Rolf replied. "He said the answer should be sent to an address in Burlington. Lonnie and I checked out the place. It's an empty office in a

14

building in the business district of town. Room 415. The superintendent says it's been empty for a year."

"That's strange," Joe commented.

"It is. No one ever goes into the place, and no mail is delivered there."

"Somebody could sneak in at night," Frank suggested.

Rolf shrugged again. "Maybe so. I'd like you and Joe to investigate that angle, too. Could you do it right away before the house burns down?"

Frank looked at Joe, and they nodded at the same time. Their father, Fenton Hardy, who was a famous private investigator, was away on a case, but he had enough confidence in his sons to let them undertake anything that came their way in his absence.

"We'll do it," Joe said. "Let's start with the driver who chased you up the road. You say he's a suspect."

Rolf gave the Hardys an odd look. "He's a suspect of sorts. But I'm half afraid to go on."

"Why are you being so mysterious?" Frank asked with a frown.

Rolf squinted. "Would you believe he's a zombie?" he muttered hoarsely.

2 *The Hessian of Hunter's Hollow*

The Hardys were dumbfounded as they listened to Rolf Allen.

"A zombie!" Joe exploded. "That's a dead person who acts as if he's alive! As if he were in a trance! Bug-eyed! That's how zombies are in horror movies, anyhow."

Frank chuckled. "It's an old superstition. Nobody believes in zombies anymore."

"Some people in the Green Mountains do," Rolf warned. "Old-timers claim they've seen the one that's rumored to have haunted our area for years. And the driver who cut me off had the blank white face of a zombie!"

"Oh, Rolf, be real," Frank said. "A zombie can't

drive a car. Tell you what. I have the license plate number. Let me check it out."

He went to the phone and called the Bayport Police Department. Chief Collig, an old friend of the Hardy family, listened to Frank's query about the mysterious blue sedan.

"Hold on," the chief told him. "I'll check the bulletins that came in today."

Frank remained on the phone until Chief Collig returned and announced, "That license number belongs to a stolen car, Frank. The owner is a farmer who lives in Hunter's Hollow, Vermont. Name's Noah Williamson. Why are you asking? Have you seen the car?"

When Frank explained, Collig chuckled and replied, "I'll have my men keep an eye out for the car, but I doubt that we'll arrest a zombie!"

Frank thanked him. Returning to Joe and Rolf, the older Hardy told them what he had learned from the police chief.

"That explains how the driver was able to follow me," Rolf commented. "I told some of the farmers around Hunter's Hollow I was coming here so they could keep an eye on our house and let me know if anything happened."

"You mean you think one of the farmers may be trying to push you out?" Joe asked.

Rolf shrugged. "I don't know. But someone obviously stole Noah Williamson's car and tailed me. When I saw him in the rearview mirror, I tried to escape, but the driver was too fast and caught up. You know the rest."

"Yes, he tried to get rid of you by knocking you into the ditch," Joe concluded. "Lucky we came along at the right moment."

Frank changed the subject. "Rolf, what's the connection between the zombie and the forest fire?"

"This," Rolf replied. He reached into his jacket pocket, drew something out, and extended it toward the Hardys on the palm of his hand. Frank and Joe could see it was a large metal button bearing the letter H indented in the center.

Joe took the button, turned it over and over between his fingers, and handed it to Frank, who gave it a similar inspection.

"What's so important about this button?" the older Hardy inquired.

"It's from a Hessian uniform," Rolf explained. "You remember, during the American Revolution there were Hessian mercenary troops fighting on the side of the British."

Joe nodded. "George Washington crossed the Delaware and beat the Hessians at the Battle of Trenton. But what's that got to do with the case?"

"The zombie is a Hessian soldier."

"Come again," Frank said, handing the button back to Rolf, who dropped it into his jacket pocket.

"The Hessians were in Vermont, too," Rolf reminded the Hardys. "The Patriots licked them in the Battle of Bennington. Well, one of the Hessians escaped. He made tracks into the Green Mountains and disappeared in Hunter's Hollow. Then some people got the idea he drowned in Hollow Brook and turned into a zombie, still wearing his Hessian uniform. They claim he fires his musket during storms, and it sounds like thunder. And the burning gunpowder starts forest fires."

"So they believe the zombie started the fire near your house," Joe surmised.

Rolf nodded. "The funny thing is that my friend, Lonnie Mindo, found the button in the cinders. You see, when the state police informed me about the fire, Lonnie and I drove to the place. There was so much smoke, I thought the house itself was burning. The firemen had their equipment all over, and they were pumping water from Hollow Brook."

"Did they keep the fire from reaching the house that way?" Frank inquired.

Rolf nodded. "After putting the flames out, they told us it was probably started by lightning or by somebody dropping a match accidentally. We scouted over the burned-out area when they left. Lonnie found the button. I took it to the Vermont University Museum in Burlington, and they told me it was from a Hessian uniform."

"Somebody's playing a trick on you," Frank declared. "He left the button where you could find it so you'd suspect the zombie."

Rolf shook his head. "How could he know we'd find the button? It was buried in the ashes. Lonnie just happened to scuff it with his toe. He—"

Rolf was cut short by a shriek in the kitchen. Frank and Joe rushed in and found Aunt Gertrude standing by the stove, pointing a ladle at the window.

"There's a stranger out there!" she cried. "A man with an ugly white face and staring eyes! He ran off when I saw him!"

"The zombie!" Frank exploded. "Come on, Joe, let's get him!"

The boys ran out the kitchen door into the darkness. A swish in the lilac bushes told them the intruder was running away in that direction. They raced after him, and saw him as he crossed their backyard to the house next door, where tall, broad rhododendrons gave him cover. He plunged between them and disappeared.

"If it weren't so dark," Joe gasped, "we'd catch him!"

"Keep going!" Frank panted. "Maybe he'll fall and we'll be able to grab him."

Passing the rhododendrons, they heard footsteps across the flagstones of the neighbors' patio. Putting on a burst of speed, Joe caught up to the fugitive at the end of the patio. He made a diving tackle, but the stranger darted to one side and ran on. Joe clutched at empty air and hit the stones with a jarring impact.

Frank rushed past, straining his eyes to see through the darkness. A tall board fence loomed ahead. He came up just as the man he was chasing vaulted up and grabbed the top of the fence. Frank seized him around the waist and pulled him to the ground, where the two wrestled over and over. Finally, Frank's adversary broke away and leaped to his feet. He drew a spray gun from his pocket and pointed it at the young detective!

At that moment, the edge of the moon appeared between the clouds. In its light, Frank saw a glaring white face with burning eyes! Then a chemical spray hit him and momentarily blinded him!

"Frank, are you okay?" Joe asked. He had resumed the pursuit after his tumble on the patio, and now paused by his brother while the fugitive scaled the fence and dropped down on the other side.

"Just got a whiff of Mace," Frank grumbled, rubbing his eyes. "Come on, maybe that creep's hiding over there!"

The boys quickly climbed the fence and ran

across another backyard into a side street. They heard a car motor starting a couple of houses away. Dashing forward, Frank wrenched the door open and turned off the ignition. As he did so, the lights in the car flashed on.

The Hardys froze in disbelief! Mrs. Schmidt, one of their neighbors, was sitting in the driver's seat.

"Frank and Joe!" she cried out. "What in the world are you doing? You had me scared to death!"

Frank gulped. "Eh, sorry, Mrs. Schmidt. We thought you were somebody else."

"A man we're looking for," Joe added.

"Do I look like a man?" Mrs. Schmidt demanded angrily. "Now, I have an appointment and I'd like to go, if you don't mind." She restarted her engine.

Frank shut the door and the car moved off down the street, turned the corner, and was lost to sight.

Embarrassed, the Hardys knew they had no chance of finding the fugitive they were after.

"He may not be a zombie," Frank declared while they were walking around the block to their house, "but he sure is a weirdo. What a face! No wonder Aunt Gertrude was scared."

They found Miss Hardy still in the kitchen in a state of great agitation. Mrs. Hardy was trying to calm her.

"He got away," Joe said in a disappointed tone.

"Too bad!" Aunt Gertrude snapped. She waved

her ladle like a club and added, "If I could have gotten my hands on him, I'd have made him see stars. Looking at me through the window like that!"

Frank chuckled. "I know you would have."

The boys went into the living room, where Rolf was still sitting on the couch. They told him what had happened, then agreed to drive back to Vermont with him the next day.

"I won't be able to go to Hunter's Hollow with you," Rolf said. "I have a rehearsal tomorrow afternoon." He handed over a key to the house, along with a card bearing the address and phone number of the boardinghouse where he was staying.

Joe pocketed both, then said, "We'd better let Chief Collig know we've been haunted by a zombie, although by now our weird friend is probably in the next state."

He called headquarters, and the chief promised to alert his whole force to look out for a stranger of Joe's description.

Then, Frank and Joe went to pack their suitcases. Aunt Gertrude, who took a dim view of their involvement in the zombie case, hovered over them with dire predictions.

"This creature you're chasing may not be a zombie, but he's certainly ruthless and dangerous. Why, he almost killed Rolf by causing an accident! I think you should leave the whole thing up to the police."

"Don't worry, Aunty, we'll be careful," Frank assured her.

"I am worried!" Aunt Gertrude said. "You—" She was interrupted by the ringing of the doorbell, and went to answer it. A few minutes later, she came back to the boys. "Frank, Joe, there's someone in the living room to see you!"

3 *Join the Circus!*

The boys went into the living room and saw a tall, thin man sitting in an easy chair. He was wearing horn-rimmed glasses and blinked his eyes as he looked at them. He rose to his feet, shook hands with the young detectives, and introduced himself.

"I'm John Tariski, director of the Big Top Circus," he said in a raspy voice. "We're on the road every summer, and we've just started this season's tour."

"We know your circus, Mr. Tariski," Frank said. "We've been to it lots of times, whenever it was near Bayport."

"The acts are great," Joe put in, "especially the bareback riders and the high-wire stunts."

Tariski frowned. "It's odd you should mention

25

those two acts. They're why I'm here. But first, I understand from your aunt that your father is away. That's unfortunate, because I have a case that I wanted him to investigate."

"Tell us about it," Joe suggested.

Tariski blinked rapidly and the rasp in his voice became more noticeable. "The Big Top Circus has been plagued by a series of accidents," he began. "But I think they're clever attempts to sabotage us."

"You mean somebody's trying to put the circus out of business?" Joe inquired.

"It looks that way. And the worst accidents could have been fatal. One of the girls who rides bareback was thrown from her horse. Then one of the high-wire performers just managed to get across before the wire snapped. Fortunately, nobody was hurt."

The boys stared at Mr. Tariski in shock, and he nodded solemnly. "The bareback rider was thrown because her horse stumbled in a hole filled with sawdust. But the hole hadn't been there the night before! And the high wire was only partially frayed. The other part was smooth, which indicated it had been filed through."

"Wow!" Joe exclaimed. "That's suspicious, all right. But have you gone to the police?"

"I went to the police," Tariski declared. "They couldn't find enough proof and suggested I hire a private detective who can travel with the circus. Actually, I doubt they believed those accidents were caused deliberately."

"But you do," Frank inferred.

"I'm convinced of it," Tariski replied. "You see, we had a succession of lesser incidents before these. The big top lights went out during a three-ring act. Also, some costumes disappeared just before a performance. But now things are becoming more dangerous. That's why I need help fast!"

"Where are you going from here?" Frank inquired.

"We're beginning our annual tour of New England. The caravan will camp in Bayport Meadow tonight and move out tomorrow morning. I came ahead in the hope of meeting your father. But I think you boys can substitute for him," the circus director added anxiously. "After all, you're detectives too, aren't you?"

"We've done some detective work," Frank confirmed.

"Well, then," Tariski inquired hopefully, "will you help me?"

Joe shook his head regretfully. "Sorry to disappoint you, Mr. Tariski, but we just took on another case. We're on our way to Burlington, Vermont."

"Burlington!" Tariski replied. "What a fortunate coincidence! The circus is leaving for Burlington

27

tomorrow. Maybe you can join us there and investigate both cases at the same time!"

Frank looked doubtful. "We'll be going on to Hunter's Hollow," he said. "I don't see how we can work at the circus. But—"

He broke off and Tariski jumped as a loud report sounded in the street.

"Was that a shot?" the circus owner cried out. "Is somebody shooting at this house? Maybe the circus saboteur is firing at me?"

Before the Hardys could answer, a number of similar sounds followed in rapid succession. Then there was a screech of brakes near the Hardy home.

Frank and Joe grinned at each other. "Relax, Mr. Tariski," Joe advised their visitor. "That's not a gun, it's a car. It belongs to one of our friends."

Frank went to the window and looked out. He saw an old jalopy careening toward the house. Smoke rose from its radiator, and its wheels appeared ready to fly off in different directions as it jolted to a halt at the curb.

The driver was a chubby youth who mopped perspiration from his face with a polka-dot bandanna. His passengers, all high-school buddies of the Hardys, were complaining loudly about the jarring ride they had had.

"It's Chet," Frank called over his shoulder. "He brought Biff, Tony, and Phil with him."

Chet Morton was the Hardys' best friend. His expansive waistline showed he was fond of eating. Although not so fond of danger, Chet had often helped the young detectives on their cases. They knew he was a good backup when they got into trouble.

Lanky Biff Hooper was a champion athlete at Bayport High. He knew how to use his fists when he waded into a free-for-all with a gang of crooks, and so did dark-haired Tony Prito, the son of a local contractor. Phil Cohen was more interested in solving conflicts with his mind, and his help had often been invaluable to Frank and Joe.

Now Chet opened the door of his jalopy. He struggled out and grinned at the others. "No problem getting to the Hardy house when Chet Morton's chauffeuring. Right?"

"Wrong!" Biff exclaimed. He had been thrown against the dashboard and then back into the seat as Chet hit the brakes. "The problem is, to walk after a ride in this heap!"

"Yes, we'll all need a pair of crutches after this!" Tony chimed in.

Chet looked indignant. "Aw, don't exaggerate. And now let's see if the Hardys are around."

"We're here," Frank called out through the front door he had just opened. "Come on in. You and the survivors."

Biff gave a mocking groan as he went up the steps. "That's just what we are. And only barely!"

The boys went inside and Frank and Joe introduced them to John Tariski. Quickly, they explained that he was the director of the Big Top Circus, and that he had come to the Hardys, hoping for their help in investigating the suspected sabotage.

"But they told me it was impossible," the man lamented. "So, I'd better be going."

Suddenly, Joe had an idea. "Look, Mr. Tariski," he said, "you need help and these guys are looking for jobs now that school's out for the summer. Why don't you hire them to work at the circus, where they can keep it under surveillance?"

"They've often helped us," Frank added, "and they're very good at this sort of thing."

"That's a thought," Mr. Tariski agreed. "I have to hire some more hands anyway. How about it, boys? Will you join the circus?"

Chet, Biff, Tony, and Phil agreed eagerly.

"What'll our jobs be?" Tony wanted to know.

"Chet likes the big cats," Biff joked. "Maybe he could be a lion tamer."

Chet gulped. "Sure, I'll handle lions and tigers," he said. "But I guess I'd better work my way up to them slowly!"

Tariski came to his rescue. "You can't have that particular job. The circus has a lion tamer already."

It was finally agreed that Chet would be in charge of the refreshment stand, while Biff helped with the maintenance. Phil would be the ticket taker, and Tony would assist the mechanic, who serviced the motors of the circus vans. Since the boy had often helped his father with the company's trucks, he had experience in that area.

"Come to Bayport Meadow tomorrow morning at the crack of dawn," Mr. Tariski told them as he got up to leave. "That's when we get the show on the road."

Chet grimaced. "Boy, that's pretty early." But he brightened up a moment later. "The circus will be fun though," Chet had to admit. "And I bet we'll catch the crook who's responsible for all this funny stuff!"

"How come you didn't take the job?" Phil asked the Hardys after Tariski had left.

"We're already on one," Joe informed him.

The Hardys described the forest fire and the clue indicating that the suspect was a zombie. The other four listened in amazement.

"I'll take the circus any day!" Chet said hastily. "Zombies! Who needs them?"

"I remember you saying very recently that you're not superstitious," Frank reminded his friend, referring to a case they had worked on called *The Four-Headed Dragon.*

31

Chet did not reply. Instead, he turned to his companions. "We'd better go home and get ready," he suggested. "I'll drop you off at your houses."

"Thanks," Phil said quickly. "But I think I'll walk."

"Me, too," Tony put in. "I need the exercise."

"Besides," Biff continued, "if we get into that rattletrap again, we might be seriously hurt and not be able to go to work tomorrow morning!"

Chet looked crestfallen. "Aw, come on, you guys," he appealed. "I got you here, didn't I? I'll get you home, too!"

Biff felt sorry for his rotund friend, who was so proud of his jalopy. "Sure, Chet. We were only kidding. We want a ride."

The four left the house, and the Hardys heard the rattling of Chet's car along Elm Street.

Early the next morning, the three boys set out for Vermont. The Hardys took their own car and Rolf said he would drive straight to the studio where he would be just in time for rehearsals.

Frank and Joe discussed the mystery on and off during the long ride. "Shall we go straight to Hunter's Hollow," Joe wondered, "and see if we can pick up the zombie's tracks?"

Frank shook his head. "While we're in Burlington, let's talk to the attorney, Tyrell Tyson. He may

32

be able to give us a clue. Then we'll have a head start when we get to Rolf's home."

The boys took turns driving, and for lunch ate sandwiches Aunt Gertrude had packed for them. They arrived in Burlington in the afternoon. The town was built on a hillside leading down to Lake Champlain, with New York State across the lake to the west, and the Green Mountains to the east. They stopped at a service station, and Frank found Tyson's number in the telephone book. Luckily, the lawyer was in his office. After hearing that the Hardys wanted to talk about the Allen house, he invited them to come and see him.

Frank drove on to the business district of town. There he parked in a municipal lot, and the boys walked to the three-story building where Tyson had his office on the second floor.

"I wonder if we'll find a clue here," Joe said anxiously before he rang the bell.

4 *The Secret Passage*

The lawyer opened the door. He had a pleasant, easy smile, and he gave them a friendly greeting. Sitting down behind his desk, he motioned his visitors to occupy a couple of wooden armchairs.

"Frank and Joe Hardy," Tyson began. "You must be the sons of Fenton Hardy, the Bayport detective. I've heard about you because of some cases your father handled for the Bar Association in Washington. Now, you say you want to talk about the Allen house out at Hunter's Hollow. Why? Clue me in," he added with a chuckle, "as I believe you detectives would say."

"Mr. Tyson," Joe began, "you're interested in the Allen house, aren't you?"

The lawyer shrugged. "I *was* interested," he confessed. "A syndicate I represent made a substantial offer for the place. They wanted to hold lectures on modern selling techniques for their executives there. However, the Allens refused our offer."

"Can you tell us anything about the forest fire out there?" the younger Hardy boy continued. "Do you think it was arson?"

"Why should it be arson?" Tyson inquired in a surprised voice. "The fire department didn't think it was."

"Someone called Rolf and said his house would be burned down if he didn't sell pronto," Frank said evenly.

"Before or after the fire?"

"Afterward."

"Probably a crank call," Tyson said. "Some nut could have capitalized on the fire. Speaking as a lawyer who handles fire insurance, I can tell you those things are not unusual."

He paused a moment and looked at the young detectives quizzically. "Why are you boys interested in the Allen house?"

"Rolf Allen hired us to investigate the fire," Frank explained. "He thinks somebody set it on purpose in order to scare his parents into selling the house."

Tyson shook his head dubiously. "My guess is, Rolf's letting his imagination run away. But if you

35

find anything wrong out in Hunter's Hollow, let me know. I may be able to give you some legal assistance."

When the conversation ended, Tyson escorted the boys to the door and shook hands. "Perhaps we can solve the mystery together," he added with a smile as he closed the door.

The Hardys decided to check out the building where Rolf had found the empty office. The address was only a couple of blocks away, so they walked over. The building was part offices, part apartments. They found the superintendent in the basement.

"What do you want?" he demanded in a surly voice.

"We'd like to see apartment 415," Frank explained. "A friend of ours used to live there and said it's vacant now. We may want to rent it."

"There ain't no apartment 415," the superintendent said. "415's an office."

"Oh, no, that can't be," Frank insisted. "Our friend wrote us a letter—"

He continued with more doubletalk until the superintendent finally said in despair, "All right, come and see for yourselves. It's just a two-room office."

He led them up the stairs, along a passageway to the office at the end. The door had a glass window with a letter chute beneath it. He unlocked the door and they went in.

They found themselves in an outer office, completely bare and covered with dust. The inner office was equally empty except for a telephone on the floor.

"Nothing but a phone, eh?" Joe commented.

"It ain't connected," the super grumbled. "Now you see it's not an apartment. You wouldn't want to rent it."

"No, I suppose not," Frank said, lingering in the inner room. He had noticed footprints on the dusty floor that proved someone had been in the place recently. But he didn't mention it.

"Our friend asked us to find out if he had gotten any mail." Joe pursued the questioning. "Did anything ever get delivered here?"

"No, of course not. There's no tenant!" The superintendent became impatient and shuffled to the door. "Have you seen enough?"

"I guess so." Joe nodded. "We'll have to get in touch with our friend and find out what happened."

The superintendent led them out of the room, locked it, and escorted them downstairs. "Shut the front door when you leave," he told them, then walked down the basement stairs in the direction of his apartment.

"He sure wasn't very friendly," Joe commented.

"And he got us out in a hurry. I wonder if he's hiding something."

Frank shrugged. "No way of telling. He could have sneaked over to Hunter's Hollow and set the forest fire. Anyhow, let's go there and see what we can find."

The Hardys returned to their car. Frank took the wheel, Joe spread a map of Vermont across his knees, and they drove out of Burlington toward the Green Mountains. Soon they found themselves in the countryside, where farms were marked off from one another by stone walls. Farmers were plowing the fields with tractors, horses and cows browsed in the meadows, and hawks wheeled in the sky overhead.

Beyond the Bolton Valley, they saw signs reading STOWE pointing northeast.

"They have some of the best skiing in the east at Stowe," Joe said. "Mount Mansfield is known to have some incredibly hard runs."

"I know," Frank said. "But tell me, which way to Hunter's Hollow?"

Joe looked at the map. "Southeast. And we should be there soon."

By now, the farming area had given way to thick woods and craggy hills. Frank turned off the main thoroughfare onto a dirt road and drove along a winding course where the car tires kicked up clouds of dust. Rounding one sharp curve, he had to brake suddenly, as a herd of deer leaped into his way from the trees on one side. When the deer pranced into a grove on the opposite side, Frank continued until they came to a sign reading DEER X-ING.

"Now they tell us!" he grumbled.

Then, all at once, he stopped again. A police car was parked in front of a driveway, and an officer was standing in the road talking to a farmer.

"Anything wrong?" Frank asked the policeman.

"No, nothing, son. I was telling Noah Williamson here that we had word this morning that his stolen car was found, that's all. A long way from here, on the East Coast."

On a hunch, Frank asked, "Was it a blue sedan by any chance?"

The officer stared at him. "How did you know?"

"We're from Bayport. Yesterday, Rolf Allen came to see us to ask our help in a mystery. We're amateur detectives. Anyway, he was forced off the road by a blue sedan with a Vermont license plate. Someone followed him all the way from here."

"You don't say!" The farmer spoke up. "You're trying to tell me someone stole my car to tail Rolf to Bayport, wherever that is?"

"That's right, as long as your license plate number is NOP 668," Joe put in.

"It is! Well, I'll be—" The farmer was at a loss for words.

"You can pick up your car at the Bayport police station any time," the officer told him. "I understand there's some damage to the right front fender. You'll have to report that to your insurance company."

The farmer sighed. "Damage, too. That's all I need." He turned to the boys. "Care to come in for a glass of lemonade?"

"Sure, we'd be glad to," Frank said.

After they had all said good-bye to the policeman, the young detectives followed the farmer into his house. Mrs. Williamson, a large, friendly woman, set out tall glasses of freshly made lemonade on the kitchen table. "What brings you here?" she inquired.

"We're going to Hunter's Hollow," Joe replied.

The farmer and his wife both looked startled by the announcement.

"What's your interest in Hunter's Hollow?" Mrs. Williamson inquired.

"We're trying to find out how the forest fire started."

An expression of dread passed over her face. "The zombie did it!" she cried. "There's been bad goings-on in Hunter's Hollow ever since that Hessian soldier came up here. Two centuries we've been

40

haunted by a dead man—a dead man who isn't dead!"

"Isn't the zombie a myth?" Frank asked.

Williamson brought his fist down on the table with a hard thump. "No!" he roared. "I saw him the day of the fire!"

The Hardys gaped at him.

"How did that happen, Mr. Williamson?" Frank asked finally.

"I was cutting wood near the Allen house," the farmer explained, "when my horse shied. I looked up, and there was the zombie running off into the trees! Oh, he's there all right!"

"How do you know it was the zombie?" Joe put in quickly.

"He was wearing a uniform. That's what the zombie wears—a Hessian uniform from the Revolution. We all know about the uniform. Blue with red borders. And that white face! Gave me a real turn, it did!"

"Go back where you came from!" the farmer's wife warned the Hardys.

"We can't do that," Frank said. "We've promised Rolf to investigate the fire."

The farmer and his wife watched in silence as Frank and Joe went out and started toward their car. A sudden sound made them turn. Williamson had wrenched the door open and was rushing out with a rifle in his hand. He raised the weapon and pointed it straight at the Hardys!

Instinctively, the boys hit the ground. A sinister rattling near Joe's elbow caused him to turn his head in that direction. A coiled rattlesnake poised to strike! Its head darted toward him and its wicked, curving fangs were about to sink into his hand!

Just then a shot rang out and the rattlesnake collapsed in a writhing heap. Williamson ran up and made sure the snake was dead. "I saw the rattler from the window," he said. "I was afraid it would bite you, so I grabbed my gun and came out. Are you all right?"

The Hardys rose to their feet. Joe shuddered. "I'm all right, Mr. Williamson," he declared. "Just a bit shaken up. You hit the bull's-eye just in time."

After thanking the farmer, the boys got in their car and drove on. They came to the Allen house, which they recognized from Rolf's description, and parked at the front door.

Behind the house, a blackened area showed where the forest fire had burned the underbrush and charred the trees. The Hardys mounted the front steps to the porch, where Frank produced the key Rolf had given them and opened the door.

They went inside and wandered through the first floor, where they found furniture covered with sheets to protect it from dust while the house was

empty. The electricity and the water were turned off. A jar of cookies stood in the kitchen on the counter beside a small Primus stove that had been used recently.

Joe pointed to it. "Looks as if Rolf and Lonnie might have stopped in for a quick meal not too long ago."

"Unless the zombie came in for a feast after starting the fire," Frank quipped. "Well, there's nothing down here. Let's see if we can find a clue upstairs."

Mounting the broad staircase, the Hardys reached the floor with the bedrooms. Narrower stairs led to a number of small rooms that once had been the servants' quarters. Dust on the landing and the floor revealed that this part of the house had been unoccupied for a long time.

The boys took a short but steep flight of wooden steps to the attic. They ended up in a single, large room under the eaves. Small windows presented a view of the Green Mountains on two sides. The floorboards creaked under their feet. A squirrel scurried out of one corner, scooted up onto a beam overhead, and chattered angrily at them.

Suddenly, Joe stopped short and grabbed his brother's arm. "Look!"

He pointed to a window. A face peered in from amid the leaves on a tree outside! It took the boys a moment to realize it was an owl perched in the tree!

"There's plenty of wildlife around here," Frank observed. "But no zombie and no clues. What do we do now?"

"We take up bird-watching," Joe suggested jokingly.

"Let's see what's in the cellar," Frank answered his own question. "That's the only place we haven't checked. If there's a clue in the house, it's got to be down there."

The boys went back to the kitchen and opened the basement door. Frank led the way down cold stone steps into a room without windows. The daylight that filtered through the open door revealed a box of candles and matches next to the lowest step.

Frank peered toward the opposite side of the cellar. "It's pitch-black, Joe. This place is way underground. Well, at least we don't have to play blindman's buff."

He handed Joe a candle, took one for himself, and lighted both with a match. Then he started forward into the darkness when Joe, who had noticed an object lying on the floor, called him back. Joe picked up the object, which proved to be a curved receptacle made of horn. An old leather strap dangled from the inner curve. The other side was indented with the letter H.

"It's a Hessian powder horn!" He gasped. "This could be a clue," he said. "Let's leave it here and see if someone comes to claim it."

"It must have been put here since Rolf and Lonnie left," Joe said, "or they would have noticed it when they switched off the electricity. See, the fuse box is in the basement, right over there."

Frank nodded. "Let's put the lights on and check the cellar out thoroughly," he suggested. He opened the metal door of the box and held up his candle. "Aw, rats," he said. "The fuses have been taken out."

"We'll have to stick to candles, then," Joe said.

"Right. You circle the room to the left, and I'll go to the right. Maybe one of us will find another clue."

"And whoever runs into the zombie first, give a yell," Joe added with a chuckle. He moved off and the darkness swallowed him up.

Frank took the reverse direction, stepping carefully and examining the floor, the wall, and the ceiling in the candlelight as he went. The dampness of the cellar made him shudder, and the eerie flicker of the candle added to the spooky atmosphere around him.

"No wonder people believe in superstitions," Frank said under his breath. "It's so lonely out here

46

in the woods that stories like the one about the zombie are bound to flourish."

Joe, meanwhile, had come to a point in the wall where the plaster had been gouged out.

Somebody used a chisel here, he thought. I wonder why.

Placing his fingertips in the crevice, he felt along the cinder blocks until he reached the top one. Slowly, he examined it for any kind of irregularity, when suddenly he reached a protruding piece of metal. As he touched it, the cinder blocks and the part of the floor he was standing on spun around!

Pitched heavily against the hard surface, Joe was carried through a secret passage to the other side of the wall! His candle went out and he was plunged into total darkness!

5 *Coffin in a Crypt*

Joe was stunned by the speed with which he whirled around. But he quickly regained his senses and drew from his pocket a pencil flashlight that was part of the detective equipment he and Frank always carried on their cases. When he snapped the flashlight on, nothing happened. A quick feel with his thumb told him that the glass and bulb inside were shattered.

Must have happened when I hit the cinder blocks, he said to himself. I hope Frank'll hear me!

Joe began to pound on the wall with the butt end of his flashlight, sending a coded signal he and Frank used when they were in trouble. He repeated it three times, but there was nothing but silence!

I hope I'm not trapped in here too long! he thought anxiously.

Sending the signal a fourth time, he finally heard a similar tapping on the opposite side of the wall. "Frank!" he shouted. "I'm in here!"

"Where's that?" came a faint response from the cellar.

"Moving platform! Cinder blocks! Trigger at top!" Joe yelled.

"I read you!" Frank called from the other side of the wall. "Hang in there, Joe!"

Scanning the cinder blocks by holding his candle up before his eyes, Frank discovered the crevice between the blocks. He followed it up to the top, where his fingers touched the trigger of the mechanism. Warned by what had happened to Joe, Frank explored carefully until he found a second button that he inferred was supposed to stop the door in the wall before it circled all the way around and closed the passageway into the cellar.

Punch the two buttons at once, he thought. That might be the control system. Let's see if it works. But I'll make sure the door doesn't close on me. I don't want to get trapped in there with Joe!

Looking along the wall, Frank saw a loose cinder block that he carried to the spot where the door in the wall opened. Then he punched both buttons and felt the floor move beneath his feet. The door

49

opened and he spun around to the other side of the wall!

Quickly, he pulled the cinder block inward, along the floor, to a spot where it would wedge the door open in case the "stop" button failed. But the control worked. The door stopped at right angles to the wall, and the passageway remained open.

Holding his candle in front of him, Frank anxiously looked for Joe. However, the younger Hardy boy was not there!

"Joe!" Frank called out. "Where are you?"

"In the cellar," came his brother's voice. Then Joe walked through the passageway. "I was caught on the moving floor again," he confessed sheepishly.

"Well, you got a free ride." Frank chuckled. "Two of them, as a matter of fact."

"You can have the third one," said Joe, laughing. "I'll give you my ticket to this fun house!"

"Where are we, anyhow?" Frank asked. "What kind of room is this?"

Joe shrugged. "Search me! My candle went out." He relit his candle from Frank's. Then they both peered around and saw they were in a small chamber with stone walls, stone floor, and a ceiling barely a foot above their heads.

There was a musty smell for want of fresh air.

Dust lay thickly on the floor. Cobwebs dangled from the ceiling, and spiders scurried away on either side.

A rectangular object stood in the middle of the room. The boys gasped when they realized it was a stone coffin!

The wall across from where they stood held plaques decorated with somber faces of men and women. Beneath each were the dates of birth and death. The first in the series read: ABIGAIL CARLTON 1775–1825.

"Frank!" Joe whispered. "We're in a family crypt! People are buried down here, but no one seems to have been here since the year one!"

"Somebody's been here," Frank muttered. "Just a little while ago. Look!"

He pointed to footprints in the dust, leading from the passageway to the coffin. They followed the marks, while their flickering candles threw an uncanny pattern of shifting lights and shadows around the crypt. Reaching the coffin, they shuddered as they saw, rudely scribbled in the dust, the words: BEWARE OF THE ZOMBIE!

Frank and Joe felt cold chills as they read the warning.

Tentatively, they placed their hands on the lid of the coffin and looked at each other.

"The zombie's been here!" Joe gasped. "Maybe that's where he hides out! Maybe he's in the coffin right now!"

An eerie feeling came over Frank. Then he shook himself to break the spell.

"We'll know in a minute!" he said grimly. "I'll lift the lid."

He placed his candle on the floor. While Joe held his where they could see, Frank took hold of the lower end of the stone lid, and slowly tilted it upward.

The coffin was empty! But the dust at the bottom was smudged.

Joe's voice dropped to a whisper again. "Frank, somebody's been in there!"

"Or some *thing*, Joe. Could be someone hid something in this coffin. There's no telling what, though."

Frank lowered the lid onto the coffin. Then he picked up his candle and looked around the chamber. "This must be the crypt of the Carlton family," he judged. "We'll have to ask Rolf about it."

"Whoever's been using the coffin must have discovered it recently," Joe commented. "The plaster between the cinder blocks was gouged out not long ago. You can tell because what's left is light compared to the rest."

After looking unsuccessfully for more clues in the crypt, the Hardys went through the opening in the wall and entered the cellar again. Frank manipulated the controls after pushing the loose cinder block into the crypt, and the movable section swung shut again.

"I can't figure out how anyone could use the crypt without being spotted by the Allens," Joe said. "It would—"

He was interrupted as a gust of wind blew out their candles. Then they heard a scuffle of feet on the stairs.

"Somebody's there!" Frank cried. "Grab him before he gets away!"

The Hardys rushed across the cellar and bounded up the stairs. At the top, they noticed that the kitchen door was open. Apparently the draft from there had blown out their candles.

Joe raced across the kitchen and looked out. A figure in a blue and red Hessian uniform was just disappearing into the woods! The figure peered back across its shoulder, and Joe saw a face glaringly white and expressionless!

"There goes the zombie!" the boy exploded as Frank joined him at the door. "Come on, let's chase him!"

The Hardys plunged out of the house, crossed the

backyard, and ran into the woods. Hoping they could head off the fugitive on either side, they split up and circled through the trees around the spot where the figure in the Hessian uniform had vanished. But when they met again deeper in the forest, neither had picked up the trail.

"We've come up empty!" Joe lamented. "There's no telling where he went. What do you think, Frank? Is he a zombie? He sure looks like one."

Frank laughed. "He looked human to me, the way he scooted off. He could run anchor man on the Bayport relay team."

Walking back toward the house, the young detectives came to the area of the forest fire. They saw burned underbrush and charred tree stumps.

"Let's look for a clue to the fire," Frank proposed.

Joe chuckled. "If I find a Hessian sword, I'll give a yell!"

They covered the blackened area without finding anything. As they passed into the unburned part, Frank bent over and plucked a small object from the grass. He examined it carefully, holding it between his thumb and index finger.

"What have you got?" Joe inquired.

"A matchbox." Frank held it up and read the label—HESSIAN HOTEL.

"The guy who dropped this may have started the forest fire," he said excitedly. "Maybe he came from the Hessian Hotel. Let's go there and scout around. The other side of the label says it's located in Hunter's Hollow."

"We didn't see it coming in," Joe noted. "Must be farther up the road."

"Yes. Let's try in that direction," Frank agreed.

They got into the car and started driving. It was already dark when they came to a large, rambling building a few miles from the Allen home. The words HESSIAN HOTEL were painted in big letters across the front.

Frank and Joe hid their car in a grove, sneaked through to the edge of the trees, and peered between the branches.

The front of the building was lighted up, and patrons were climbing the steps to go in. The rest of the hotel was dark.

"Looks as if they don't use the back rooms," Frank said. "I wonder why."

"Let's find out," Joe suggested.

Cautiously circling the building, they saw that the rest of the windows and the back door were boarded up. Suddenly, a car drew to a stop in the trees at the rear. A man climbed out, walked behind a tall oak, and vanished from view.

The Hardys hit the ground and crawled across the clearing to the oak. Carefully looking around on either side, through the bushes at its base, they were staring directly at the boarded-up rear door of the Hessian Hotel! The man, however, was nowhere in sight!

"He must have gone around the corner," Joe said in an undertone.

Before Frank could answer, another car halted amid the trees. The driver approached the back door and rapped on one of the boards, first four times, then three, then two.

The door, boards and all, swung open! A burly doorman admitted the visitor, then closed the door behind them.

"It's a blind!" Frank whispered. "They only pretend the place is boarded up!"

In the next ten minutes, the Hardys watched a number of new arrivals gain entrance by rapping the same signal on the board. Each time, the burly man opened up silently, pointed down the corridor, and closed the door.

"He's telling them where to go," Joe said. "Frank, I bet they're a gang of crooks and this is their hideout!"

One more man arrived and entered as the others had. The doorman was about to go in after him, when Joe moved to stretch his muscles. A fine film of pollen drifted down on him from the bush overhead.

He breathed in a mixture of air and pollen, and

his nose twitched. Desperately, he raised his hand to stop the irritation. Too late! He sneezed loudly!

The doorman heard the noise. He swung around and glared in the direction of the oak tree. With upraised fists he strode toward the bushes where the Hardys were hiding!

6 Trapped!

Frank and Joe prepared to defend themselves as the burly doorman advanced menacingly toward them. They were about to jump to their feet when another man came around the corner of the building.

"Grimm!" the newcomer called in an undertone. "The door's closed. I have to get in for the meeting. Hurry up!"

Grimm turned around. "Musta closed by itself," he grumbled. Returning to the door, he unlocked it with his key and let the man in.

The Hardys made a dash for the woods while this was going on. Looking back through the trees, they saw Grimm return to the oak and beat through the bushes. When his search proved fruitless, he shrugged as if to say he must have been mistaken, and went back into the Hessian Hotel.

"The crooks are having a meeting in there," Joe whispered. "What can we do about it, Frank?"

"Go in the front and look around," Frank decided. "We don't need a signal to get in, and perhaps we'll find a clue to what goes on in the back."

The young detectives circled the building, climbed the steps, and went into the hotel. They found themselves in a vestibule leading to a ball-room. A headwaiter was showing patrons to their tables.

The boys spotted Grimm in a corner, talking to a man in evening clothes. Grimm had his back to them. "You're the concert director, Pollard!" he said angrily. "And you better get things going pronto!"

"My two guitarists haven't shown," Pollard complained. "They sent their guitars ahead, but now we have nobody to play 'em. How can we do a country and western concert with just a singer and a bass?"

"That's your problem!" Grimm snarled. He strode into the ballroom without noticing the Hardys, and went through a door at the rear.

But Pollard saw the boys and came toward them. "Are you the guitarists?" he asked querulously.

Frank thought quickly. "We do play guitar," he admitted, referring to the fact that he and Joe often performed in student concerts at Bayport High.

"We're ready to play now," Joe offered.

"What took you so long?" Pollard demanded. "The agency said you'd be here on time!"

Joe continued the cover-up. "We had to find Hunter's Hollow."

"It's our first trip to this area," Frank added.

Both boys were thinking that they were really telling the truth without giving themselves away.

"Well, go in and get the music going," Pollard replied irritably. "What are your names?"

"Frank and Joe," Frank replied.

Pollard nodded and led the way into the ballroom, which had a broad dance floor with a platform for musical performances at one end. Long black drapes hung down over the windows. The illumination was soft, but strobe lights flashed intricate color patterns around the room.

A blond singer on the platform was waiting, holding a microphone in her hand, and a bass fiddler was tuning his instrument. A couple of guitars lay on chairs at the rear of the platform.

Pollard made the introductions. The singer was Kate Fuller, an attractive woman in her late twenties. The bass fiddler was George Stephenson. Both wore jeans and plaid shirts. Kate had a white western-style hat on her head.

After introducing them, Pollard said, "I know none of you have played together before. So, do the best you can. Kate, you take it from here." The concert director walked back to the vestibule.

Kate looked at the Hardys. "Where are your jeans?" she queried.

"We didn't bring them," Frank informed her. "We didn't know we'd need them. There's nothing we can do about it now."

George grinned. "Yes, there is. Try the dressing room behind us."

In the dressing room, Joe slid the door of a long closet to one side. The boys saw an array of stage costumes lined up on coat hangers, blue jeans and plaid shirts among them.

They quickly selected a couple of pairs and changed into them. Frank had a pretty good fit, but Joe's shirt was too big. The cuffs of his sleeves extended halfway down the palms of his hands.

"I feel like I'm in a tent!" he complained.

"Just make sure the cuffs stay up when you're playing," Frank said cheerfully.

"No way. I'm going to find a shirt that fits me," Joe said. He began sliding the costumes on the coat hangers along the bar that held them. Finally, the last outfit emerged from behind the other door of the closet. It was a blue and red Hessian's uniform with the top button of the coat missing!

"The zombie's here!" Joe gasped.

"I doubt he came for the concert," Frank replied.

"He's probably in the back of the hotel. We have to find him if we can."

George poked his head in. "Come on, guys!" the bass fiddler called out. "We have to start."

The Hardys followed him. "Joe," Frank said in an undertone, "we'll get in the back when the concert's over. We know the signal. Let's just hope the real guitarists don't show up and spoil our act!"

Reaching the concert platform, they joined George and Kate, who explained the numbers on the program. "I'll come in on the solos," she said. "Frank, you'll join me for a duet, if you've got the voice."

"I can get by with it," Frank informed her. "Anyway, with you here, nobody will notice me."

Kate smiled at the compliment. Then she continued, "Joe, you have a solo guitar."

Joe plonked the strings of his instrument. "I'm ready," he replied.

The concert began with Kate giving her rendition of a ballad called "Riding Down the Trail." She sang in a clear soprano voice, catching the loneliness of the Old West:

> *Riding down the trail*
> *When the sun is setting low,*
> *Heading for the bunkhouse*
> *When there's no place else to go.*

When she finished, the audience applauded enthusiastically. Several more songs followed. There was a brief intermission, and then the concert resumed. Kate and Frank did a bouncy tune for their duet, called "Montana Mountains."

Then Joe came on with his solo guitar. Pulling the right cuff of his shirt up above his wrist, he began to play the hit tune of a popular western group. The force of his fingers hitting the strings caused his cuff to slide down over his wrist. Down and down it slipped over his palm, interfering with his thumb and making him hit a wrong note. The audience tittered. Desperately Joe moved his arm over his head. He shook his hand violently. The cuff fell back above his wrist. He immediately attacked the guitar in a flurry of twanging strings and ended with a flourish. The audience cheered.

Frank chuckled. "Joe, were you playing the guitar or doing arm exercises?"

"Both," Joe grumbled. "This stupid shirt almost made me sprain my thumb."

After the concert, the Hardys went back to the dressing room and changed into their regular clothes. Putting their costumes on the hangers, they noticed that the Hessian uniform was still there. Frank took it down and they inspected it.

"No clues besides the missing button," Joe observed. "It's got to be the button Rolf showed us."

63

Frank replaced the uniform in the closet and closed the door. "We'll leave the outfit where it is. That way, whoever put it here won't know we spotted it."

When the Hardys returned to the ballroom, the audience was breaking up. Kate and George said good-bye and left the hotel. Pollard paid Frank and Joe, then they, too, went out. But instead of driving off, they ducked into the shadows and sneaked around to the rear of the building. Keeping the back door under surveillance, they saw another man rap the signal and go in.

"The meeting must still be going on," Joe muttered. "Let's knock and see what happens."

"Okay. But be ready for action. These guys look like they play rough."

The brothers walked out of the woods, and boldly approached the door. Joe rapped four times, then three, and finally two. The door opened, and Grimm, the doorman, glared at them.

"I ain't seen you guys before!" he snapped suspiciously.

"This is our first time. We're on special assignment," Joe said.

"We know the signal," Frank spoke up. "The boss thought that was good enough to let us into the meeting. Isn't it good enough for you, Grimm?"

The man gave them an uneasy look. "If the boss

64

wants you to attend, I'm not gonna keep you out. Go on in."

The Hardys entered and the door slammed shut behind them. "Go down the corridor to the middle room on the right," Grimm growled. "The one that's lit."

The boys walked along the dismal hallway, past a flight of stairs leading up to the next story. They could see a door at the end of the corridor connecting the ballroom to the back part of the building.

"Well, we're in," Joe whispered. "What we're in *for* is what bugs me."

"Play it by ear," Frank cautioned.

The room they entered was lit by a dim bulb in the ceiling. A dozen men were gathered around a radio. One of them kept spinning the dial to keep static from interfering with the reception. The young detectives stopped near the door to listen. No one noticed them.

They heard a strange, squeaky voice. "Now I've given you the details, I expect you to carry out the plan. All goods are to be stored in the attic of the Hessian Hotel. Be extra careful when you deliver."

The voice paused for a moment. The Hardys realized they had stumbled into a gang of thieves. Apparently, the leader was giving them their orders over the radio!

The squeaky voice resumed talking. "We'll tame the lions tonight."

Frank nudged Joe. "Must be a code," he whispered.

"Let's see if he lets on what the code means," Joe whispered back.

But they were disappointed to hear the squeaky voice conclude: "That's all for now."

Suddenly, the door to the ballroom banged open. Pollard's voice roared down the corridor. "The guitarists just got here! Those two kids who played were impostors!"

Frank and Joe ran from the room. Since Pollard blocked any escape through the ballroom, they rushed to the back door. However, Grimm was hustling toward them and the gang members were piling out of the room after them at the same time! They were trapped!

Pollard and Grimm were just about to grab the Hardys when Joe leaped to one side onto the stairs they had passed coming in. Frank followed. They took the steps two at a time up to the darkened second floor of the hotel. The men pounded after them!

Frank pulled Joe against the wall. They stood there, panting for breath, and let the gang go hurtling past.

"We can double back down the stairs and get out

the back door!" Frank gasped. "The way we came!"

They started toward the top of the stairs, only to freeze as Pollard called from the darkness of the hallway: "Grimm, stay in the corridor in case they try to escape down the stairs!"

The Hardys stopped short. Joe's foot scuffed against the bottom step of a flight of stairs leading upward. "This way!" he whispered.

He and Frank rushed up the stairs. A door rose in front of them at the top step. Frantically, Joe felt across it until his hand closed over the knob. Then he opened the door and the boys stepped into the room.

Joe closed the door behind them. He fumbled around until he discovered that he could fasten the door by dropping a wooden bar into metal slots on either side of the opening.

Meanwhile, Frank was playing the beam from his flashlight over the interior, which was obviously the attic of the Hessian Hotel. They saw boxes and bales bearing manufacturers' names piled high toward the ceiling. According to the labels, they held such things as cameras, toasters, and stereo equipment.

"These are the stolen goods Squeaky Voice mentioned on the radio," Frank judged.

Just then, they heard the sound of feet thumping up the stairs toward the attic. Fists began beating on the door, and the crooks yelled threats at the Hardys.

"Open up!" Pollard bellowed. "You can't get out of the attic anyway, so you might as well give in!"

"Not yet!" Joe muttered. He ran over to a window where a streak of moonlight showed between the boards covering it. The glass panes were gone. He kicked the boards out with his heel. Poking his head through the window, he saw a straight drop to the ground.

"We can't escape this way!" he exclaimed in despair.

The men outside battered the door furiously, until the bar holding it started to splinter. It was only a matter of moments before the door would give way.

"We're trapped!" Joe groaned.

7 Mysterious Footprints

"Maybe not!" Frank exclaimed. He had been shining his light across the ceiling. "There's a skylight up there, and bales of stuff are piled right under it! Maybe we can climb up."

Getting a toehold on the lowest bale, Frank clambered from one to another until he reached the top of the pile. The skylight was grimy with dirt, but he managed to force it open.

He started to climb through as Joe reached the bale below him. Just then, the attic door burst open, and the crooks poured through.

"They're at the skylight!" Pollard thundered. "After them!"

Frank levered himself through the opening onto

the roof. The thieves ran toward the bales and began to climb up. One of them was stretching to seize Joe by the foot as the boy was getting out. But Joe held onto the edge of the skylight, swiveled to one side, and kicked the top bale over. It tumbled down the pile, carrying the gang with it onto the attic floor.

Quickly, Joe squirmed through the skylight and joined Frank on the roof.

"See if there's a way to the ground," he cried out. "A downspout or something."

"Must be a drainpipe over there," Frank said, pointing to a corner where two gutters came together from either side.

They slid down the roof and braced themselves against one of the gutters just as the first of the gang climbed through the skylight.

"There they are!" the man shouted to his companions, and started over the roof toward the Hardys. Five others followed.

Frank and Joe expected to escape down the drainpipe. But when they leaned over the edge of the roof, they saw it extended only about ten feet below the gutters. The rest of the spout had fallen away, and there was no possibility of climbing down!

Frantically, the boys ran in the opposite direction behind one of the gables, or pointed sections, of the

rambling roof. Stooping low, they moved through a cramped area, then turned left behind another gable. The gang gathered where they had just been.

"Which way did they go?" Pollard snarled. "Left or right?" Nobody knew. "Okay, split up and cover both ways. Push 'em to the edge of the roof! If they fall over the side, it's a long way down! It'll save us the trouble of doin' 'em in!"

Frank and Joe ran from their hiding place. The only way to go was toward the last gable. Scrambling over, they caught Pollard's eye. "We got 'em!" he exulted, ordering his men to resume the chase.

The Hardys slid down the gable onto a flat part of the roof. Rushing to the edge, they discovered nothing except a tall tree whose branches did not extend to the roof. Again the gang converged on them!

In the nick of time, Frank noticed a sturdy branch sticking out from the trunk about six feet below them and the same distance from the wall of the building. Desperate, he leaped into space, grabbed the branch as he fell toward the ground, and swung into the tree. Joe did the same, escaping from the roof just before the crooks reached him.

"Follow 'em!" Pollard screamed at the man in the lead. "Follow 'em, Magnus!"

"Not on your life!" Magnus exploded. "The

branch is too far from the roof! I'd only break my neck!"

Pollard yelled at the others, but none would jump from the roof to the branch.

The Hardys, meanwhile, had scrambled to the ground and were running to their car as fast as they could.

"Let's go back to Rolf's house and phone the state police," Joe panted as he slid into the passenger seat. "That squeaky voice we heard must be the same one that warned Rolf to sell the house!"

It was shortly after midnight when the boys reached the Allen house. A strange car stood in the driveway, and Noah Williamson and three other men came down the steps as Joe braked to a halt. All four waved ax handles in a threatening manner.

"Uh-oh, we've got a welcoming committee!" Frank muttered. "And they don't look very friendly."

Williamson ordered the Hardys to get out of their car. The three men with him gathered around and scowled at the boys.

"We've been waiting for you," the farmer growled.

"What do you want with us?" Frank inquired.

"You'll find out when you get to my place,"

Williamson replied. "Come on! One of you in each car. Move!"

Frank was forced to take the lead in their yellow sports car, with one of the men beside him and another in the back seat. Williamson rode in the second car, guarding Joe.

They turned in at the Williamson farm and came to a stop. Frank and Joe were escorted into the house. Mrs. Williamson was in the front room.

"You'll have to stay here till the police arrive," she informed them.

The Hardys stared at her in amazement.

"You mean we're wanted by the police?" Frank's voice revealed his disbelief.

The farmer's wife nodded. "They told us to keep you here till a squad car comes."

"What's the charge?" Joe asked.

"Helping the zombie!"

Frank was incredulous. "Did the police say that? Look, call their headquarters. They'll tell you it's all a big mistake."

Mrs. Williamson shook her head. "No need to," she said emphatically. "It was the police who called here."

"Wait a minute," Frank continued as a thought struck him. "Was it a squeaky voice on the phone?"

Mrs. Williamson looked surprised. "You're right about that," she admitted.

"That wasn't the police!" Frank exclaimed. "That guy's the leader of a gang of crooks! He wants us out of the way! That's why he said for you to grab us at the Allen house and bring us here! But I wonder how he knew who we were?"

"Who is he?" Williamson demanded.

Frank shrugged. "We don't know," he confessed.

Williamson scoffed at them. "I think you're making the story up. Maybe you two are crooks! Anyway, it'll be settled when the squad car comes here."

"Might be some time," his wife told him. "All the cars are tied up with an accident on the Burlington road. We'll have to wait for the first one that's free."

"Don't try to escape from this house," Williamson warned the boys. "There are four of us, and we'll be watching the doors and windows."

The men went out of the room and Mrs. Williamson followed.

"Pollard warned Squeaky Voice that we got away from the Hessian Hotel," Joe recounted. "And Squeaky Voice phoned Williamson, pretending to be the police and asking him to nab us at the Allen house. Who is he, though?"

"Obviously he knows our connection with Rolf," Frank pointed out. He got up and made a tour of the room, looking at the door and windows. Williamson was sitting in a wicker chair on the front porch, and

Mrs. Williamson was in the kitchen. The three other men were watching at the side windows. Frank returned to Joe and sat down.

"We've got to get out of here," he said in a low tone.

"But how?"

"I have an idea. Listen."

Frank explained his plan, which Joe agreed to. They waited until they heard Mrs. Williamson's footsteps descending the stairs into the basement. Frank took from his detective's kit a noise pellet that exuded red smoke when it exploded. Then he ran through the kitchen and opened the back door. He pressed the self-destruct button, and hurled the pellet high over the nearest trees into the woods.

A loud explosion followed. Red smoke rose from the underbrush, visible in the porch light.

"What was that?" Williamson shouted while Frank returned to the front room.

"A fire!" one of his companions yelled. "The underbrush is burning!"

"Keep it from reaching the house!" Williamson bellowed.

He rushed through the kitchen and into the backyard. The Hardys, meanwhile, ran out the front door into the driveway. Joe opened the hood of Williamson's blue sedan and the car that had brought Joe, and disconnected some of the wiring. Frank slid behind the wheel of their car, and, as soon as Joe jumped in, gunned the vehicle out onto the road. They roared off to the Allen house in a cloud of dust.

When they arrived, Joe phoned the state police and told the sergeant at the desk about the Williamson incident.

"We didn't make that call," the sergeant confirmed. "But we'll send a squad car to Noah and see what it's all about."

"Thanks," Joe said and gave the sergeant a description of the crooks at the Hessian Hotel.

The policeman sounded skeptical. "The Hessian Hotel has a good reputation," he protested. "And I've met Pollard there. He seems like a reputable concert director."

"The ballroom's a front," Joe insisted. "Pollard runs a criminal operation in the back."

"Okay, we'll follow it up." The phone went dead.

"What now?" Joe asked as he put down the receiver.

"We search the house again," Frank declared. "The zombie may have come back while we were away."

As in their first investigation of the place, they did not find a clue upstairs. They then descended into the cellar, lit candles, and entered the underground crypt. The lid of the stone coffin was tilted to one side onto the floor!

"Frank, you were right!" Joe exclaimed. "The zombie's been here!"

The boys stared into the coffin and saw the Hessian powder horn lying on top of a piece of paper. On the latter were scrawled the words:

HARDYS, THE ZOMBIE IS WATCHING YOU!
GET AWAY WHILE YOU CAN!

Frank put the paper in his pocket. "We'll ask him for an explanation when we catch up with him," he grumbled.

"Frank!" Joe cried suddenly. "Maybe we interrupted him! Maybe he's still hiding in the cellar right now!"

They quickly ran back into the basement and went off in opposite directions to head off the zombie in case he was concealed in the darkness. Frank moved to the right, holding his candle to light his way. Turning when he came to the corner of the wall, he continued on until he reached the furnace.

He heard a rustling sound behind it and could dimly see somebody moving in the darkness! Frank placed his candle on the floor, ducked under a large pipe, and hurled himself at the figure!

78

"Hey!" a familiar voice cried out. "Take it easy, will you?"

"Joe!" Frank exclaimed. "I thought you were the zombie!"

"My candle went out," Joe explained. "I was going to ask you for a light when you jumped me!"

They scouted through the cellar and found nothing, so they finally went upstairs again.

"I vote we stay here tonight," Joe suggested. "We can go to Burlington tomorrow and ask Rolf about the crypt. Maybe Lonnie knows something he's not telling."

Frank shrugged doubtfully. "Let's sleep in the front room. If the zombie comes back to the house, we'll be ready for him."

The boys found covers in the linen closet, and put them on the couch. Then they took turns sleeping and watching for the zombie. Joe was on guard when suddenly thunder boomed overhead and rain began to patter through the open window. A flash of lightning illuminated the front porch.

Joe saw a figure in a Hessian uniform standing at the open window! As he stared at the grisly white face, the figure made a threatening sweep with its arm!

Joe woke Frank with a shout. "It's the zombie! On the porch!"

Frank leaped to his feet and followed his brother

out the door. They barreled through onto the porch.

"Where's he now?" Frank asked.

"No way of telling," Joe answered in disappointment.

While they were straining their eyes and ears in the darkness, another bolt of lightning flashed across the sky and they saw the figure rushing into the woods.

Instantly, the Hardys ran down the stairs and across the yard. But once in the woods, they realized pursuit was hopeless in the darkness and the rain. They returned to the house for the rest of the night. In the morning, when the rain had stopped, they went out into the woods again.

Frank pointed to a set of footprints in the mud. "That's the way he went!"

Joe shivered. "It's the track of the zombie!"

8 *The Hermit*

The mysterious footprints ended in the underbrush beyond the muddy patch.

Frank was disappointed. "That's it for tracking," he said. "I wonder what he was up to."

"Maybe he wanted to start another forest fire and the rain stopped him, so he decided to pay us a visit," Joe ventured.

When they got back to the house, he pointed to something on the living room floor and exclaimed, "Wait a minute! This wasn't here yesterday!"

He picked up a paper wrapped around a rock and held in place by a rubber band. Detaching the paper, he flattened it on the table. The Hardys saw crude lettering similar to that on the message in the stone coffin. It read:

HARDYS, GET OFF THE ALLEN CASE.
FINAL WARNING!

"The zombie must have tossed the rock through the window last night when I saw him move his arm," Joe inferred. "Frank, he sure is trying to scare us! This case is getting more and more dangerous!"

Frank nodded. "I wonder what the police found," he said and went to call headquarters.

"The back of the Hessian Hotel and the attic were completely empty when we got there," the sergeant informed him. "No crooks, no stolen goods. Pollard says he can't imagine why you told us that story. He thinks you're crazy."

"Did you find the Hessian uniform in the dressing room closet?" Joe persisted.

"No. The closet was empty, too!"

"The zombie was at the Hessian Hotel," Joe said to Frank after he hung up. "He took his uniform for last night's caper. Then Pollard kept us out of the way at Noah Williamson's long enough so we couldn't blow the whistle on the gang while they moved the hot goods out of the place." He sighed. "Well, Rolf seems our best bet now. Let's talk to him."

The Hardys drove to Burlington, and were invited by Rolf to come up to his room in the boarding-house.

"Lonnie will be here any minute," the boy stated. "He went to the library to read up on Shakespeare. We're rehearsing different plays at the studio, so we usually come and go at different times. Today I'm back earlier than usual. How's the investigation coming?"

Frank and Joe took turns explaining what had happened to them since they arrived at Hunter's Hollow.

"I told you the zombie was mixed up in it!" Rolf exclaimed.

"Somebody who wears a Hessian uniform, anyway," Frank observed.

"He does look like a zombie," Joe admitted.

Just then Lonnie Mindo came in. He was a friendly youth who smiled and said he was pleased to meet the Hardys.

"I'm due at the studio after lunch," he declared. "We've been rehearsing *Julius Caesar* all week. I'm playing Caesar, and I get assassinated in the third act." He grinned.

"That reminds me of something we found," Joe said, and asked about the crypt with the stone coffin.

Rolf shook his head in amazement. "I never knew about that! The Carltons must have had it put in when they built the house. I suppose it was forgotten after they sold it."

"Did you know about the crypt, Lonnie?" Frank inquired. "You were living in the house."

"No, but I wish I did. It must be fun to find a crypt with a stone coffin. Spooky!"

"What will you do now?" Rolf asked the Hardys.

"Try to find another clue," Joe replied. "We have to identify who was in the crypt."

"I have an idea," Lonnie put in. "I've heard about a hermit named Burrows who lives in the Green Mountains. He's supposed to have occult powers, and knows everything that goes on. Why don't you talk to him?"

"Maybe we should," Frank answered. "How do we find him?"

"They say he lives in a cave near the top of the tallest peak due east of Hunter's Hollow. Say, I'd better have lunch and get over to the studio. Want to come along?"

"Sure," Frank said, hoping to have a little more time with Lonnie. "We'd like to see a rehearsal."

"I'll come, too," Rolf declared. "I've memorized my part, so I'm free this afternoon."

The four went to a fast-food restaurant and had lunch. Over their hamburgers, they discussed their acting experiences.

"Lonnie, did you ever play a Hessian soldier?" Frank asked.

Lonnie chuckled. "Never. I always play a Patriot in plays about the Revolution. I like to be on the winning side!"

After lunch, the four strolled over to the studio. The director was showing a number of actors how to move around the stage. Lonnie joined the cast and Frank, Joe, and Rolf took seats in the front row.

The group was to rehearse the third act of Shakespeare's play, the assassination of Julius Caesar amid a crowd of Roman senators in the Capitol of Rome. Before they started, the director hopped down from the stage and approached the Hardys and Rolf.

"We need more senators for this scene," he said. "How about you boys filling in? You know the play, don't you?"

"We studied it in English class," Frank confirmed. "I'll be glad to give you a hand."

"Me, too," Joe offered. "Do we have to wear sheets?"

"Roman togas." The director chuckled.

A few minutes later, the Hardys and Rolf, decked out in togas from the wardrobe department, were watching the actors who portrayed such famous Shakespearean characters as Brutus and Cassius.

The assassins attacked Julius Caesar, portrayed by Lonnie, with rubber daggers. He tumbled to the floor as red ink spattered over his toga.

After rehearsal, the director came into the wardrobe department where the Hardys were removing their togas.

"Thanks for filling in," he said. "You did just fine."

"No problem," Frank replied. "It was fun."

"Lonnie's an excellent Julius Caesar," the director added. "He has great potential."

"Has he been here for all the rehearsals this week?" Joe inquired casually.

"Yes, he's been here every afternoon," the director confirmed. "Well, I'd better get back to the stage. The play doesn't end with the assassination of Caesar. We have a couple of hours to go yet."

"I guess that lets Lonnie off the hook as a suspect," Joe commented after the director had left. "He was rehearsing here in Burlington while the zombie was trying to scare us off the case."

"And we have no proof Lonnie knew about the crypt in the Allen house," Frank added. "But who was in there, then? I hope the hermit can give us a lead."

Frank and Joe accompanied Rolf and Lonnie back to the boardinghouse, where they all spent the night. In the morning, the Hardys drove into the

Green Mountains. Then they headed for the tallest peak east of Hunter's Hollow. The road became narrower until at the base of the peak they had to park in the woods and proceed upward on foot. Suddenly, the trail ended. They had to push through a wild area of large trees and thick underbrush that slowed their progress, and could no longer see the peak.

"We'd better take a bearing before we get lost," Frank suggested. He climbed a lofty pine tree, spotted the peak, and the two resumed their trek up the mountain.

"This certainly is the right place for a hermit," Frank muttered. "You want isolation, you got it."

The tall trees thinned out near the top, where the boys came to a rocky area marked by steep ledges and boulders scattered in the underbrush.

A grating sound made them look up. To their horror, a huge boulder was rolling down the mountainside! Gathering speed, it hurtled directly at them!

Frank and Joe dived to either side, hit the ground, and somersaulted out of the way. The boulder tumbled down between them, and they heard it crashing down into the underbrush below.

"If we'd been hit," Joe gasped, "we'd have gone over like tenpins in a bowling alley!"

Frank nodded. "How come it came so close? Seemed like someone aimed it at us!"

"Someone did, Frank!" Joe pointed toward the mountain peak where a man was peering down at them from the mouth of a cave. He had long, matted hair, a scraggly beard, and wore a tattered corduroy shirt and dungarees.

"He must be Burrows," Joe continued. "And I'm sure he pushed that boulder at us."

"I guess he doesn't like company," Frank muttered. "I hope we can get him to talk."

As they resumed their advance upward, the hermit shouted harshly, "Go back!"

"Mr. Burrows, we want to talk to you!" Frank called out.

"I don't talk to nobody," the man yelled, tugging at another boulder in an effort to loosen it.

The Hardys leaped onto a ledge leading to the summit of the mountain. They moved so quickly that Burrows had no time to aim the rock at them, and he ran into his cave.

Entering after him, they found the hermit brandishing a club. They noticed the primitive living conditions. Berries and fruit were piled in the rear of the cave. A jug of water was standing on a stone that served for a table.

"What do you want?" the hermit shouted with a wild look.

"Some information," Joe said. "We were told you know everything about the mountains."

"You can help protect the mountains from more forest fires," Frank pleaded.

The hermit appeared mollified by Frank's remark. He dropped his club and began to babble about uncanny forces in the woods.

Suddenly, he turned toward the mouth of the cave. The Hardys heard a rustling sound in a maze of heavy underbrush.

"He's there!" the hermit cried triumphantly. "I knew he'd follow you!"

"Who—" Joe began as he wheeled around, but he never completed his sentence.

9 An Odd Confession

The bushes parted. A squirrel darted out, scooted past the Hardys, and raced up a tree on the other side. A lynx bounded after the squirrel. Seeing the Hardys, the lynx twisted around and flew back into the bushes. It could be heard retreating into the underbrush down the mountainside.

The boys relaxed and grinned at one another.

"Fooled by a lynx," Frank said.

"Well, we saved a squirrel," Joe replied.

They went back into the cave where Burrows was waiting for them.

"The lynx is my friend," the hermit said with a leer. "He watches anyone who comes into the mountains. He followed you here."

Ignoring the hermit's comment, the younger Hardy boy firmly repeated that he and Frank were interested in a forest fire.

"I know all about it!" the old man interrupted him. "I can show you. Follow me."

Before they could say anything more, he strode out of the cave. Galvanized by the thought that they might find the solution to the Allen case, Frank and Joe trailed him on a march through the woods. They had to force their way between saplings, and briars clawed at their legs. The hermit maintained a fast pace, muttering to himself, but the Hardys stayed close to him.

"Where is he taking us?" Joe queried in an undertone.

"Let's just hope he solves the forest fire mystery for us," Frank whispered back.

They came to a narrow ledge where the side of the mountain faced a sheer drop into a valley below. Seeming not to notice the danger, Burrows stepped rapidly along the ledge to the opposite side. The Hardys followed, using their training in mountaineering techniques to keep their balance.

"He's risking his neck," Frank complained. "And ours, too!"

"What he's got to show us better be good after this hike," Joe muttered.

Suddenly, the hermit turned and shouted loudly.

It startled Joe so much that he lost his balance! His foot slipped, and he plunged off the ledge!

Lunging forward, Frank caught his brother's jacket and pulled him back. Breathing heavily, they maneuvered their way to safety and rejoined the hermit.

"What were you shouting about?" Frank demanded.

"I wanted to make sure you boys knew where I was," Burrows explained. "I didn't see you and thought you were lost."

"We almost did get lost, taking a swan dive off the ledge," Joe said accusingly.

Burrows shrugged. "Do you want to know about the fire or not?"

"Yes, we do. That's what we're here for. So let's get on with it."

"Then keep up with me," the hermit said. "I won't bother waiting for you anymore."

They went forward in silence until they reached a deep, narrow gorge where a plank was thrown across to permit hikers to get to the other side. The Hardys and their guide stepped along the plank and walked down the mountain for a couple of hundred yards.

Burrows stopped and pointed with his finger. "There's the fire!" he exclaimed.

The Hardys looked in the direction he indicated. They saw a small, blackened area where flames had charred trees and bushes within a circle of massive boulders. The splintered trunk of an oak lay across a pile of rocks.

Frank and Joe felt disappointed as they looked around.

"This fire was started by lightning," Frank said. "The bolt hit that tree."

"Sure," Burrows retorted. "You said you wanted to know about a forest fire. Here it is."

Joe shook his head. "That's not the fire we mean. We're interested in the fire near the Allen house in Hunter's Hollow."

Burrows became angry. "Did we come all the way out here for nothing?"

"You didn't let us finish the question," Frank pointed out. "We didn't get a chance to say which fire it was. We thought you must have guessed. That's why we followed you."

The hermit smirked. "I'll tell you about the Allen fire when we get back to the cave," he promised.

"Why not now?" Joe asked, but Burrows didn't answer.

Retracing their steps, they reached the plank over the gorge. Burrows went first and the Hardys followed. They were in the middle of the board when he stepped off. He looked at the plank, then bent down and lifted it, twisting it so violently that Frank teetered and lost his footing. With a scream, he fell, but managed to catch the board with his hands. Desperately, he hung on to keep from dropping to the bottom!

Joe, who was almost at the end, stepped off when Burrows started to lift the board upward. He tore the plank from the hermit's grip and lowered it back into place. Frank got one foot up, then pulled himself to safety. A moment later, he too was on solid ground.

"You did that deliberately!" Joe accused Burrows. "You tried to knock us into the gorge! Why?"

"What are you talking about?" the man protested. "The board had shifted and *I* was about to drop off. So I tried to anchor it again so you boys could cross safely, but then it slipped in my hands. I was only going to help, and now you accuse me of trying to kill you. That's what the world is like: no gratitude anywhere. I'm glad I don't have to live with other people anymore. They're all alike—greedy and ungrateful and—"

"Never mind," Frank said harshly, interrupting his rantings. "Let's go back."

Burrows turned abruptly and resumed the trek to the cave. The Hardys followed.

"I don't trust this weirdo," Joe declared. "He's trying to get rid of us—*permanently*. There's no telling what he'll do next."

Frank nodded. "But we have to go along. He just might give us a clue to the Allen mystery."

Both boys watched the hermit closely when they came to the ledge where Joe had nearly gone over the side. However, Burrows never looked back. Instead, he conducted them to his cave in silence.

When they were inside, Frank looked him straight in the eyes. "All right. Now you know which forest fire we mean. Tell us about it."

The hermit nodded with a cunning grin.

"Who started the fire?" Frank pressed.

Burrows gave a high-pitched cackle. "I did!"

Startled, the boys stared at him. They waited for him to continue. Instead, he began to munch a handful of berries.

Finally, Frank broke the silence. "You stay up here in the mountains all the time, don't you?"

"Sure do," Burrows said. "I like to be alone and close to my cave. I told you what I think of people—"

"Then how did you set a fire miles away down in Hunter's Hollow? Why did you go there?"

"I didn't!" the hermit exclaimed. "I didn't go near Hunter's Hollow!"

Joe was irritated. "You're not making sense. What do you mean, you started the fire but you weren't in Hunter's Hollow? Whoever started it had to be there!"

"I told my partner to start the fire," Burrows informed them. "So I'm responsible, too. Is that so hard to understand?"

"Who's your partner?" Joe asked. "Who are you working with?"

"The zombie!" Burrows croaked. "The Hessian soldier! You know about him, don't you?"

"All right," Frank said soothingly to humor him. "The zombie started the fire. The guy in the uniform. But who is he? Has he got a name?"

"Ask him if you want to know!"

"We will, as soon as we catch up with him," Frank said. "Where can we find him?"

"There!" cried the hermit, pointing to the mouth of the cave, where a shadow seemed to be gliding by.

The Hardys rushed outside. Quickly, they surveyed the area, but nothing moved in the bushes or the underbrush. There was no sight or sound of anyone coming toward them through the trees.

"Another false alarm," Frank stated, disappointed.

"Wait a minute!" Joe exclaimed. "Look! Down there!"

He pointed into the distance. They had a broad view far over the Green Mountains into Hunter's Hollow, and gasped at what they saw.

Smoke was rising over the woods in the vicinity of the Allen house!

10 Raging Flames

"It must be another fire!" Joe exploded. "We'd better get there and alert the fire department!"

Without another word to the hermit, the Hardys plunged down the mountainside, tripping and stumbling over creepers, digging in their heels at each jump to keep from falling.

Finally, they came to the trail leading to their car. They jumped in and roared back to the Allen house. When they came closer, they ran into a roadblock set up by the Vermont State Police.

"There's a forest fire up ahead," an officer called out. "The area is cordoned off. It's touch and go whether we can save the Allen house."

"We're friends of Rolf Allen," Frank stated. "May we go through?"

"Not unless you volunteer to assist in putting out the fire," the patrolman warned.

"We'll be glad to volunteer," Joe said quickly.

"Okay." The patrolman moved the roadblock. "Go ahead. They can use all the help they can get. Tell Captain Scott I sent you. He'll show you what to do."

The boys drove through and parked within sight of the Allen home. The fire was on the other side, so they ran around the building. The dense smoke made them cough, and they saw angry tongues of flame shoot up among the trees. Leaves were fluttering to the ground from fire-scarred branches. As the boys watched, a tall tree, its trunk nearly burned through, fell over onto its smaller neighbors.

"What an inferno!" Joe exclaimed. "I've never seen anything like this!"

Five engines from Burlington were lined up in the yard, and pickup trucks stood nearby holding machines for spraying antiflame chemicals. Some firemen were hosing down the fire, while others were using bulldozers to clear away the underbrush.

Still others were attacking burning trees with

chain saws to make them topple into the conflagration instead of the unburned areas. A helicopter clattering overhead released streams of chemical spray at the most dangerous points.

Members of the state police mingled with firemen in a scene of incessant activity. Finally, the boys found the man in charge.

"Are you Captain Scott?" Frank asked.

"I sure am, but I can't stop to talk. I've got my hands full."

"We're volunteers," Frank said.

"Oh, that's different. Report to the fire chief over there, Chief Bemont. He'll give you your assignments."

The fire chief handed the Hardys a couple of hard hats and shovels. "Join the gang on the firebreak in front of the house," he instructed them.

The firebreak was a wide swath a number of men were cutting through the underbrush in the path of the fire. "The flames will have nothing to feed on when they reach the firebreak," Bemont explained, "if we get it dug in time. So, get going!"

The Hardys moved into place at the end of the line. To their surprise, the digger next to them was Lonnie Mindo!

"I was at the boardinghouse when the police phoned about the fire," the boy explained. "Rolf was at a rehearsal, so I called the studio and left a

100

message for him. Then I came barreling out here to do whatever I could."

While they were talking, Rolf arrived. He thanked Lonnie for his quick reaction when the fire alert came in. Then he turned to the Hardys.

"Frank and Joe, that includes you, too," he said. "I just hope we can save the house."

Chief Bemont added Rolf to the crew digging the firebreak, and work continued at a feverish pace. A fireman in a bulldozer marked out a line by pushing bushes and undergrowth to one side. The men wielding shovels and pickaxes were then able to cut through the grass. They tossed the sod to one side, exposing the bare earth.

The heat was intense, and wisps of smoke drifting out of the fire made everyone's eyes water. Their arms ached and their breath came in spasmodic gasps.

Joe was at the end of the line in front of the house. Seeing a burst of flame shoot through a gap the bulldozer had missed, he rushed forward to beat it out with the back of his shovel. At that moment, a shower of red-hot embers fell behind him, starting another blaze. He ran for the open space between them, but the flames met and cut him off!

Joe was trapped, his cries for help lost in the roaring and crackling! Desperately, he attacked the smoldering underbrush with his shovel, but the

flames shot even higher! Step by step, they forced him back toward the burning trees, where he was about to be engulfed by the raging inferno!

Luckily, Frank noticed in time that Joe was caught. He dropped his shovel, dashed to a pickup holding a chemical machine, and leaped in. Gunning the pickup forward, he jolted to a halt just across from Joe. He twisted the nozzle frantically and sent a heavy shower of chemicals over the nearest flames, thus cutting a path through the fiery circle. With a cry of relief, Joe stumbled to safety.

"Are you okay?" his brother asked him anxiously.

"I feel like a fried egg. Otherwise, I'm fine. Anyway, thanks for the spray. It saved my life!"

A fireman approached. "Those chemicals are being held in case the house catches fire," he said sternly. "You shouldn't be using them down here!" But he complimented Frank after hearing about Joe's close call.

Then the Hardys moved back into the line working on the firebreak.

"We need more hands!" an officer called out.

"They're on the way," the chief responded. "In fact, here they come."

Two trucks rolled into the area, disgorging volunteers. Frank and Joe were too occupied to notice the new arrivals until they heard a familiar voice. "Hey, Hardys!"

The speaker was Chet Morton. He was accompanied by Biff, Phil, and Tony! They greeted Frank and Joe, who introduced them to Rolf and Lonnie.

"How did you get here?" Frank asked.

"We'll tell you later," Biff replied, since the fire chief was already handing them hard hats and spades and assigning them to the firebreak in front of the house.

A small plane flew overhead and a moment later two red parachutes blossomed in the sky. Chet pushed back his hard hat. "Those guys will get toasted!" he predicted.

"No, they know what they're doing," Joe said. "They're smoke jumpers. They'll land in a place the fire hasn't reached and keep the flames from spreading."

"I think they'll use explosives," Frank spoke up.

The parachutes disappeared into a green area of untouched trees to one side of the fire. Moments later, a series of explosives proved Frank was right. The smoke jumpers were dynamiting trees that would catch fire if they weren't removed from the path of the blaze. Their efforts stopped the fire in that direction.

Meanwhile, the flames in front of the house licked their way through the vegetation as far as the firebreak. Reaching the bare earth, they went out.

Water and chemicals doused the last of the burning embers. Only smoke and charred vegetation showed where the fire had raged.

"That does it," the fire chief called out finally. "It's under control. Let's take the engines back to Burlington."

The volunteers piled into the trucks, which moved off. Firemen rolled up their hoses, stowed their gear, and climbed aboard their vehicles. The heavy fire engines lumbered off, leaving deep ruts in the yard of the Allen house. The pickups with their drums of chemicals followed.

Chief Bemont and Captain Scott conferred. They agreed the area was now safe. "I'll have the road-blocks removed," Scott said and left.

Bemont walked over to the boys and congratulated them. "You all did a great job," he said. "Rolf, your house is safe. It was a shift in the wind that caused the fire to move. It began off in the woods and should have burned out over there."

"How did it start?" Frank inquired.

The chief frowned. "I think somebody deliberately set it. We found several burned matches under a bush. Seems the bush wouldn't catch fire, so the arsonist moved on to some dry underbrush."

"He should be put in jail!" Lonnie exclaimed hotly.

"He will be," Bemont promised, "if we can identify him." With that, the chief went to his car and drove away.

Rolf and his companions were left alone. All were blackened by soot. They had minor burns, bruises, and blisters, and felt exhausted.

"Fellows, let's go inside and get cleaned up," Rolf invited the others.

Minutes later, they were taking showers and dabbing antiseptic cream on their hands and arms; then they went downstairs to the front room.

"How about some food?" Rolf suggested.

Chet grinned and patted his stomach. "You're talking my language, Rolf. Make mine an apple pie. A whole apple pie!"

Chet's friends from Bayport chuckled. They knew Chet liked eating better than anything else.

"Sorry, Chet." Rolf grinned. "I don't have apple pie. But we can see what's in the pantry. I know we have cocoa."

Chet raised his hand in a lofty manner. "Say no more," he intoned. "I'll take whatever you have."

Trooping into the kitchen, the group soon produced the edibles. Then they moved out onto the porch, gathered chairs, and sat down.

"Phil, now tell us how you got here," Joe inquired. "We thought you were with the circus."

"We are with the circus, Joe. The caravan's on the road to Burlington. The state police stopped us and asked for volunteers to fight the forest fire."

"So we came here in a truck," Tony added. "But we have to get back soon."

"We'll have to return to Burlington ourselves," Rolf said. "But before we go, why don't we check out the crypt the Hardys discovered? I can't wait to see it!"

"Crypt?" Biff asked, puzzled.

"In the basement," Joe said. "Seems none of Rolf's family knew about it."

When they had finished their meal, they all trooped downstairs and lit candles.

"There was a box of fuses for the electricity when we left the house," Lonnie pointed out. "Now they're gone."

"No doubt someone took them on purpose to keep us in the dark," Joe grumbled. He led them in a single file across the cellar. Lonnie was at the end of the line. The candles the eight boys carried threw an eerie light in the room, and the only sound was the scuffing of their shoes on the cement floor.

Reaching the secret passage, Frank explained how the movable segment of the wall operated. He pushed the two control buttons, and the cinder blocks moved inward. The floor at the base of the blocks shifted in the same direction, carrying Frank through into the crypt. The moving blocks came to a halt halfway in, leaving the secret passage open.

"Come on in," he invited the others, "and see how the zombie lives!"

Joe entered first. The increased number of candles lit up the room, and the Hardys could see more clearly than before how the tombs of the Carlton family were built into the opposite wall. The stone coffin glinted in the candlelight. Cobwebs dangling from the ceiling swayed in the draft created by the open passageway leading into the cellar.

"A weird place to choose for a crypt," Tony said, brushing some cobwebs out of his hair.

Chet nodded. "The zombie can have it!"

As the boys looked at the coffin, the door of the secret passage moved silently behind them. No one noticed they were about to be trapped!

11 Circus Caper

A loud thump at the entrance to the crypt made them whirl around. The swinging door was wedged against a cinder block, which had prevented it from closing.

"We were almost caught in here!" Joe gasped. "The way I was the first time!"

"How did the cinder block get there?" Biff wondered. "It stopped the door."

"I pushed it into place with my foot," Frank revealed. "I knew it was next to the door because that's where I left it. But what started the control mechanism? I know I set it right."

He ran to the door and pulled it open. Lonnie was standing outside looking very confused.

"Did you hit the button?" Frank asked him.

"I must have touched it accidentally," the boy replied, "when I lifted my candle so I could see to follow you in. I didn't even know it was there."

"But didn't you see Frank set the controls?" Joe inquired.

"I couldn't. I was at the end of the line, remember? Anyway, I would have figured out how to open the panel again if it had shut."

"Lonnie wouldn't scare us like that deliberately." Rolf defended his friend. "You don't think—"

"No, of course not," Joe said soothingly, but the suspicion about Lonnie Mindo lingered on in his mind.

Frank felt the same way, but did not want to pursue the matter any further. "Let's lift the lid of the coffin and see if the Hessian powder horn is still there," he suggested, and explained to the others how he had taken the warning note, but left the powder horn.

Biff and Lonnie moved the cover and everyone stared in surprise. "It's gone!" Joe exclaimed. "The zombie came back for it!"

Frank nodded. "Too bad we didn't catch him."

"We saw a zombie," Chet spoke up. "I don't know if he's the same—"

"Where?" Frank inquired in a startled tone. "Around here, Chet?"

"At the circus. The sideshow has a zombie act. Fellow named Bones Arkin. He's quite good. You should catch his act. Best in the sideshow."

"Check him out," Tony added. "He may be your suspect."

Biff nodded. "Arkin could have sneaked away from the circus when he was off duty. He could have shown up here to haunt you."

"But he couldn't have been the same guy who followed Rolf to Bayport," Joe objected. "The circus wasn't here then."

"Maybe he has an accomplice," Phil spoke up. "Why don't you come back with us? The caravan's just down the road. Besides, we need help with the sabotage mystery. We haven't discovered anything yet."

Everyone agreed to Phil's suggestion, and when Rolf and Lonnie left for Burlington, Frank and Joe followed the truck driven by Tony. Soon a large van came into view. It was lettered on the side, BIG TOP CIRCUS. The rest of the caravan stretched out in front of it by the side of the road.

The Hardys stopped at the office van while their four friends went back to their jobs.

"We'll work on the sabotage angle," Frank proposed before they went in. "That'll make a good cover while we're investigating Bones Arkin."

Joe agreed. "We don't want anyone to know why we're interested in his zombie act."

John Tariski greeted them as they entered the van. He blinked rapidly behind his horn-rimmed spectacles as he listened to their offer to stay with the circus for a while and see if they could solve the sabotage mystery.

"Excellent! Excellent! We can't have accidents happen to the circus while we're on this tour," he responded.

The raspy sound of his voice suddenly struck Frank. Was his the disguised voice on the telephone? the boy thought. He could talk with a squeak if he wanted to. But why would he purposely invite us to investigate? And why would he sabotage the circus?

Aloud, Frank said, "We'll mosey around the place and see if we can find a clue. Can you arrange it so we won't be stopped?"

"Of course. I'll see you boys have the run of the circus. I'll tell my ringmaster, Whip MacIntyre. Ah, here he comes now."

MacIntyre was a tall, elegant figure. He wore a black top hat, a white silk shirt, a scarlet coat, white riding breeches, and leather boots. He carried a short whip and had a habit of striking his right boot with it.

Tariski introduced the Hardys and added,

"They're investigating the accidents we've been having."

MacIntyre smiled. "Mr. Tariski tells me you boys are first-class detectives," he said. "That's good, because we need pros on this case. But we can't tell anyone why you're really here. That would only alert the culprit. You need a cover. What shall it be?"

"Say we're reporters writing a story on the circus," Joe suggested. "No one will suspect us."

MacIntyre slapped his boot with his whip. "That's a good idea. You can move around and ask questions, and nobody will be suspicious. You see, we're dealing with a clever criminal, so I'll give you boys all the help I can." He turned to Tariski and added, "The four hands we hired in Bayport have returned from fighting that forest fire in Hunter's Hollow, so the caravan is ready to roll again."

"Good. Tell the drivers to get going, then," Tariski instructed him. "We need to make up for lost time."

"Will do," MacIntyre responded. "Well, I'll see you boys later." He left the office and they heard him shouting orders to move out.

"We'll follow the caravan," Joe told Tariski. Then he and Frank went to their car. Soon they were rolling down the road toward Burlington.

The circus was home for all those belonging to it.

The equipment was carried along everywhere, including the big top that gave the circus its name. This was the enormous tent that covered three rings for simultaneous performances, and was tall enough for the trapeze and high-wire stunts.

At every curve in the road, the Hardys could see the whole caravan. First came the office van from which Tariski handed out printed sheets advertising the circus. Next in line were the vans holding the cages of the big cats, the bears, and the elephants. There was a special glass-lined cage for snakes, after which came monkeys, and horses for the bareback riders. After them, followed by the equipment van, were trucks in which the manual laborers bunked, and the trailers in which the performers lived.

"It's a town on wheels!" Joe marveled as he counted the vehicles. "We could put everybody in Bayport aboard those vans."

"We should do it at the next football game," Frank joked. "It sure would solve the parking problem at the stadium."

The caravan wound its way through the Vermont countryside. Trees extending over the road swept their branches along the roofs of the vans, and leaves tumbled down. Birds flew higher and perched in taller trees. Rabbits, squirrels, and woodchucks scurried away at the sound of the approaching motors.

As the caravan passed through small towns, the people came out to watch. They lined the streets, laughing and shouting. Parents held their children up for a look at the performers and the animals. Many in the crowd waved at the Hardys, who brought up the rear in their car.

Joe chuckled. "They think we're in the circus, Frank."

"Sandow the strong man and Leo the lion tamer!" Frank joked.

"I'd rather be a clown," Joe decided. "That's what I was in our last Bayport variety show. I'll stick to the makeup and the baggy pants. It's safer than playing with lions."

The caravan reached a detour where the road was under repair, and turned onto a dirt lane where it proceeded through a haze of dust. Suddenly, the lead vans came to a halt, forcing those in the rear to stop, too. The Hardys heard shouting up ahead. People were leaning out of the windows to see what had happened, but nobody seemed to know.

After a few minutes of waiting, Joe said, "Let's find out what the trouble is."

He and Frank got out of the car and walked along the caravan to its head. There they realized what was causing the delay. The van holding the big cats was stuck in a large hole. One of the rear wheels was just about to come off the axle.

"What happened?" Frank asked Tony Prito, who was the driver of the van.

"I'm stuck in a hole and one of my rear wheels is about to fall off," Tony grumbled.

Tariski looked upset. He blinked his eyes and rubbed his hands together. "What rotten luck!" he gasped. "And we're behind schedule already. We have to move on!"

Biff, Phil, and Chet got tools and with the help of the hydraulic jack managed to secure the wheel. Then they began digging around the rear of the van. Finally, they gave Tony a signal to try to pull the vehicle out. But the wheels continued to spin.

After a while, Biff straightened up and rested his shovel across his shoulder. "It's no use. We need to tow it out."

MacIntyre was standing nearby, watching them. "A tow is no problem," he declared. Turning toward a van near the middle of the caravan, he shouted: "Bring Leah up here!"

"How can somebody named Leah give us a tow?" Chet mumbled.

Joe pointed toward the elephant van. "There's your answer."

The elephant trainer brought one of his animals out of the rear of the van to where the big cat van was stuck in the mud. Then he fastened two heavy chains on either side of a broad leather harness

116

across the shoulders of the elephant. Tying the opposite ends of the chain to the van, he shouted: "Forward, Leah!"

She leaned her weight against the harness. The chains tightened, and she began a slow walk forward that caused the vehicle to move. It came halfway up out of the mudhole to the cheers of the spectators.

Just then, the left rear wheel tilted high in the air. It had careened onto a big rock hidden by the mud. The right rear wheel at the same time sank deeper than ever. "Keep going, Leah!" the trainer yelled. The elephant strained against her harness, when suddenly one of the chains snapped! The van swiveled to one side and pitched over at a crazy angle, threatening to fall on its side.

The jolt caused the bolt on the rear doors to snap back. One door fell open. So did a door of the tiger cage inside, and two tigers leaped toward the opening!

12 *Tiger Terror*

The spectators screamed and ran away from the van.

"The tigers will escape!" MacIntyre shouted. "Close that door!"

Phil was already running forward. He slammed it shut and forced the bolt back into place. The two big cats collided with the door, making it shake. But the bolt held fast under the impact.

"The tigers are still loose in the van!" MacIntyre yelled. "We've got to get them back in the cage!"

Biff took a food container from the storage compartment, grabbed a piece of meat, and tossed it through the window of the van into the tiger cage.

The striped cats bounded after it, and Biff was able to reach through and relock the cage doors.

"Good work!" Phil complimented his friend.

MacIntyre nodded vigorously. "You both deserve credit for quick thinking. All right, let's get the van straightened out."

Chet went to the equipment vehicle and returned with a new chain. He fastened one end to the elephant's harness and the other to the van's bumper.

"Leah! Once again!" the trainer called. The elephant moved forward, pulling the rear wheels clear of the mudhole. The van, moving over the stone, righted itself.

Tony examined the wheels and found that nothing was damaged. Relieved, he climbed back into the cab, and the caravan resumed the drive to Burlington. Because of the delay, the circus arrived after dark. The vans camped in an open area outside the city.

Tariski summoned the members into a circle. "This is where we'll set up the big top," he informed them. "The sideshow will be to the right, and the entrance where we'll sell tickets just beyond. Be ready first thing in the morning."

The crew and performers began cooking their dinner. Frank and Joe went forward and joined their

Bayport pals. As they all carried hot dogs and soda under some trees where they could discuss the situation, the Hardys explained that they were posing as newspaper reporters.

"That loose wheel and the broken chain were no accident," Chet pointed out. "Someone loosened the lugs so that the wheel would come off when it hit the first pothole, and I bet the chain was tampered with to give under stress. I reported it to the elephant trainer, but he didn't believe me."

"Probably the same guy who staged all the other accidents did it," Joe delared.

Frank shrugged. "Could be more than one person, Joe. Maybe a gang's involved. And what about the bolts on the van and the cage? How could both of them open at the same time?"

"I think that was sabotage, too," Phil replied. "There was nothing wrong with the bolt on the van door. It just wasn't properly fastened."

"Same thing with the bolt on the tiger cage," Biff put in. "Someone deliberately slipped it open and waited for the so-called accident to happen."

"It must be an inside job," Joe declared. "Only someone connected with the circus has a chance to commit sabotage that often."

Suddenly, a dry stick snapped in the darkness amid the trees! There was a rustle of footsteps in the underbrush!

"Somebody's over there!" Frank said in an undertone. "He's trying to hear us! Keep talking! We'll grab him if he comes closer!"

The boys began to discuss writing newspaper stories on the circus. The footsteps approached cautiously and stopped behind a nearby bush. At that point, Frank stood up and said he was going back for more soda. Moving toward the bush as if to pass it, he suddenly turned, leaped over it, and landed on a man crouching on the other side. The two went down in a heap. Biff came to Frank's aid, and together they hustled their captive into the open. He was a small, wiry man with lanky black hair.

"It's Bones Arkin!" Chet exclaimed. "The circus zombie!"

"Why were you hiding there?" Frank demanded. "Are you shadowing us?"

"I wasn't hiding and I'm not shadowing anyone," Arkin protested. "I couldn't sleep, so I decided to take a walk in the woods. How was I to know you boys would be holding a powwow under the trees? I was tying my shoelace when you jumped me!"

Seeing the uncertain expressions on the boys' faces, he addressed Frank and Joe. "Hi, there. I heard you're reporters covering the circus."

The Hardys nodded and introduced themselves.

"We intend to catch your act," Joe added.

"Best in the sideshow!" Arkin boasted. "Gives 'em the chills!"

Frank chuckled. "We'll let you know our opinion after we see the snake charmer."

"Well, you can interview me any time," Arkin offered. He yawned and stretched. "The walk made me sleepy. I think I'll hit the hay."

He strolled of in the direction of his van.

"Think he's telling the truth?" Biff asked his companions.

"That's what we'll have to discover before this case is over," Frank said grimly.

The boys broke up after that. Frank and Joe borrowed sleeping bags from Biff, who had charge of the circus gear, and spread them on the ground next to their car.

"Wait a minute," Joe said. "That broken chain's bugging me. Chet said it was nearly filed through. Suppose more equipment's been sabotaged!"

"There's one way to find out," Frank declared. "Let's go to the equipment van and check everything before they start using the stuff tomorrow!"

"Right now?"

"Sure. Why not?"

They walked down the long caravan, which had fallen silent for the night. Stopping at the equipment van, they pulled the door open and climbed inside. Frank took out his detective's flashlight. Its beam revealed a line of boxes marked by content from horseshoes to tent poles and strands for the high-wire act.

The Hardys inspected the boxes one by one.

"Everything looks in order," Frank muttered.

Then his flashlight beam fell on a single chain lying in a corner. Joe picked up one end and tested the edge with his thumb.

"Frank, it was filed all right! Part of the edge is as sharp as a knife! That chain wouldn't have held a baby carriage for very long!"

At that moment, a big flashlight snapped on outside the van! A broad ray flashed into their faces, forcing them to shield their eyes with their palms.

"Who are you?" a voice snarled. "What are you doing in there?"

It was Whip MacIntyre. The boys dropped their hands, and he recognized them.

"Frank and Joe Hardy!" he exclaimed. "I suppose this is part of your investigation. Have you found anything?"

The boys squatted on their heels at the van door. Joe held out the end of the broken chain.

"This!" he replied. "This chain didn't break accidentally."

MacIntyre inspected the cut link. "I agree," he declared. "This is just terrible. I hope you find out who's responsible."

With that, the ringmaster walked off, and the Hardys returned to their work in the van. They went into a corner where boxes were stacked containing bigger props such as the seesaws used by the tumblers and the cycles ridden by the trained bears. The young detectives inspected them all carefully.

"Everything's okay except the broken chain," Frank finally said. "And they won't be using that anymore."

They were turning away from the corner when they heard something hissing in the darkness just behind them. A slithering sound on the floor came closer and closer. Frank lowered the beam of his flashlight and gasped.

A mean-looking boa constrictor was crawling toward them!

Hemmed into the corner of the van by the boxes, the boys had no room to edge past the snake. It glared at them with its horrid reptilian eyes, and began to coil itself to strike at Frank, who was holding the light.

Frantically, Joe ran his hands over the boxes in the hope of finding a weapon with which to strike the boa constrictor. "Keep it occupied, Frank!" he gasped. "I'll see if I can find a shovel or a crowbar!"

"Make it fast!" Frank grated. "The flashlight's the only defense I've got. And it's too small to stop a snake this big!"

Joe's fingers clasped around a burlap sack. Taking it down, he opened it and maneuvered it forward. The boa arched its neck, opened its jaws, and struck viciously at Frank.

But Joe pushed the sack in between them. The force of the thrust caused the snake to propel half of its length into the sack. Quickly, Joe tilted the burlap container upward so the entire serpent would fall in. Then he twisted the neck of the sack. His hands were shaking, but he sighed with relief.

"Joe, you should be a snake charmer!" Frank said admiringly. "I sure didn't want to get into a hassle with that critter!"

"Maybe I ought to join the circus sideshow." Joe laughed. Then he added seriously, "How did that thing get in?"

"Somebody put it here," Frank surmised. "They don't let boa constrictors crawl loose around a circus. This one was intended to attack us. Joe, the saboteur knows who we are! He noticed my flashlight in the van and saw a chance to sic the snake on us!"

"But how did he get in? Let's visit the snake charmer in the morning and see if she can tell us."

Finding a length of rope, Joe tied the neck of the sack. He and Frank carried the snake to their car, where they deposited it on the back seat. Then they crawled into their sleeping bags and soon were fast asleep.

When they awoke at sunrise, the snake was gone!

They rushed to the van bearing on its door the words: REPTILIA, THE SNAKE CHARMER. A woman answered their knock, a small boa constrictor wound around her neck. The young detectives drew back instinctively, realizing at the same time that the snake was not the one that had almost attacked them.

"Uh—you must be Reptilia," Joe stammered.

"That's right," the woman replied brightly. "Better known as Jill Morgenstern from Milwaukee. But who are you? I haven't seen you around before."

The Hardys introduced themselves as reporters covering the circus.

"Did you happen to lose anything last night, Reptilia?" Frank asked casually.

"Like what?"

"Like the daddy of your friend there," Joe said. "A bigger boa constrictor."

"No, of course not. It's still in its cage. Come on, I'll show you. But why do you ask?"

While Frank explained, the snake charmer conducted the Hardys to a glass box. A big boa lay coiled inside. A stick with a hook and drawstring for lifting it out stood beside the box.

"This one's too vicious to use in my act," the woman told them. "So I put it on display. Sells a lot of tickets to the sideshow."

"Could someone have taken the boa out during the night," Joe asked, "without your knowing it?"

"And put it back before you got up?" Frank inquired.

"Could be," Reptilia admitted. "The box stays out front here, while I sleep in the back with the door closed. And it's easy enough to lift the snake with that hook. But why would anyone want to do that?"

"You tell us," Joe suggested.

"I can't!" she retorted sharply. "Are you accusing me of letting the snake loose?"

"Oh, no, we're not accusing anyone," Joe said soothingly, but Reptilia was not mollified.

"I've got to get ready for my act. You'd better leave."

The Hardys walked over to the main circus area.

"That boa constrictor has to be the one that came after us," Frank observed. "I had a pretty good look at it while you were finding the sack. The markings are identical. Besides, it's apparently vicious enough to have done the job it was meant to do."

Joe nodded and reconstructed the incident hypothetically. "Let's see now. The saboteur saw your flashlight in the equipment van, being close enough to recognize us. Then he went to Reptilia's van and took the snake out of the glass box with the hook while she was asleep. He probably carried it away in a sack. Anyway, he sneaked up to the door and let the snake loose."

Frank nodded. "He must also have watched you maneuver the boa into the sack, and followed us back to the car. Then he took the snake and replaced it in the glass box in Reptilia's van before she woke up. But who is he? Who knows who we are?"

"Tariski and MacIntyre," Joe pointed out. "The director and the ringmaster of the circus. Also, other members might have found out about us by eavesdropping on our talk with Tariski. Like Bones Arkin. He sure looked like he was listening to us when I pounced on him."

Frank looked frustrated. "That's the trouble, Joe! We have too many suspects!"

13 *Danger on the High Trapeze*

The entire circus was awake by now. The tents and sideshow stalls were going up amid furious activity. Some of the men hammered stakes into the ground to hold the guy ropes. Others spread the canvas over the grass and decided where the poles should go. Wild-animal cages rolled into place. Poles, wires, and trapezes lay to one side, ready to be set up for daring stunts high in the air. The horses of the bareback riders stood tethered to a tree.

Tariski walked around shouting encouragement. "The show opens this afternoon! Get everything ready! Raise the big top!"

The director's last order referred to the enormous tent lying folded in the middle of the open space.

Six men levered steel poles into sockets driven into the ground. Two elephants moved into position at opposite ends of the big top, and the rigging connected to the poles was attached to their harness. The six men, assisted by many more, unfolded the tent until it covered the elephants and dropped onto the grass on the other side.

Ordered to go forward in opposite directions, the huge animals pulled the rigging, causing the poles to move upright and pushing the canvas into place. It was quickly anchored to guy wires on the outside. Then the workers placed rows of benches for the spectators along both sides. They marked out the three rings on the grass and set up the equipment used by the performers.

The Hardys pitched in to help Biff and Tony, who were on the work gang.

"The big top's ready," Biff commented as they finished the center ring. "But I have to check the equipment for the acts."

"And I have to check the pickup that carries the cages from the vans," Tony said. "Can't have the motor conk out when the tigers are in the back."

Whip MacIntyre approached and inspected the center ring. "Good," he said, slapping his whip against his boot. He walked away through a crowd of performers who were practicing their acts. Girl bareback riders were doing handstands as their horses cantered around the tent. Acrobats were bouncing off a seesaw into a chair atop a tall pole. A high-wire daredevil was balancing himself on his wire by manipulating a pole held parallel to the ground.

"No sense staying here," Frank said to Joe. "We'll only be in the way. Let's mosey over to the sideshow."

"Chet and Phil are there," Joe noted. "We can see what they're doing."

The sideshow was a smaller tent divided into stalls for the various acts. Passing the sword swallower and the fire eater, the Hardys came to where Reptilia was allowing her pet boa constrictor to wind itself around her arm. The glass box holding the other, more vicious serpent stood on the counter in front of her. The snake charmer ignored Frank and Joe as they passed by.

"We're not her favorite people," Frank observed. "I wonder if she's guessed why we're here."

Joe shrugged. "She *could* be a suspect, Frank. How do we know somebody took her snake during the night? *She* could have put it in the van. Nobody better with snakes than a snake charmer!"

Frank sighed. "I know."

They found Chet and Phil at the concession

131

stand. Phil was sitting in a chair counting several rolls of tickets, while Chet was fitting a wire mesh for hot dogs and hamburgers into the top of his grill.

He grinned at the Hardys. "Too early, fellows," he said. "I'm not open for business yet."

"Don't eat up all the business yourself," Joe kidded him.

Chet winked. "Why not? That's why I took the job."

"Do you know anything about Reptilia?" Frank asked his two friends.

Phil shuddered. "I'm not going anywhere near her. Not with those critters around. What's your interest in the lady?"

Frank described how he and Joe had been threatened by the boa in the van during the night.

"So Reptilia is a suspect," Phil concluded. "And even if she's innocent, I hope we can stay clear of her snakes!"

Leaving their pals to their duties, the young detectives walked back along the sideshow, turned the corner, and continued along the rear of the stalls. Suddenly, a canvas was whipped aside, and a weird soldier dressed in a Hessian uniform came toward them! He seemed in a trance. His face glistened an unearthly white, and his eyes never blinked! He showed no expression, but his hands clutched at the boys!

132

The Hardys were too astonished to move. Frank had goose bumps, and Joe felt a cold shiver go down his spine.

The hands of the weird soldier reached toward their throats and then clapped each of them on the shoulder.

"What's wrong, guys?" he said. "Don't you know me? I'm Bones Arkin."

The Hardys relaxed. They grinned ruefully at the thought of being startled by a sideshow performer.

"This is my zombie act," Arkin went on. "Pretty good, no?"

"Pretty good, yes," Joe admitted. "You scared me half to death. Where'd you get the costume?"

"And what gave you the idea of portraying a zombie?" Frank added.

Arkin laughed. "I change my outfit wherever the circus goes. Last place we stopped I was a vampire. Here, I decided to be a zombie because of the legend of Hunter's Hollow."

"We've heard of it," Joe stated. "Have you ever been to Hunter's Hollow?"

The sideshow performer shook his head. "I'm not looking to meet a real zombie. Which reminds me, I'd better get on with my practicing for the grand opening this afternoon." With that, he went back into his stall and closed the canvas curtain.

"Is he telling the truth?" Frank wondered. "I noticed his uniform has all its buttons."

"So did I," Joe replied. "But he could have sewn a new one on after getting back from Hunter's Hollow. If he *went* to Hunter's Hollow."

After lunch, people began streaming into the circus area. They formed a long line at the ticket booth, where Phil counted the money handed to him, gave back change, and passed out tickets.

Chet stood behind the concession stand, calling, "Peanuts! Hamburgers!" He wore a chef's hat and a white apron, and kept turning hamburgers and hot dogs on the grill with a long fork.

Frank and Joe strolled over to him and watched him open a roll and insert a hot dog. He handed it to a boy who walked away munching it with relish.

"Chet, you should be a chef," Frank said with a chuckle.

"I know," Chet replied. "I think I'll get a job at the Bayport Diner. After this, I'll be a pro."

The Hardys followed the crowd past the sideshow toward the big top. They arrived when the grand parade began.

A band, playing a stirring march, led the parade. MacIntyre followed, dressed in his finery and waving his whip at the spectators. A couple of clowns came along, each carrying a monkey on his shoulder. Jugglers and acrobats were next, followed by the high-wire and trapeze artists. Children screamed with delight and adults applauded when the bareback riders rode in. Then came the elephants, the trained bears, and the big cats rolling by in their cages.

Biff and Phil joined the Hardys. "I'm scheduled to check the high trapeze," Biff said. "MacIntyre told me to do it in the intermission between the grand parade and the first performance."

A few minutes later, he walked across the arena to a tall ladder, and climbed to a small platform high above the ground. A trapeze was fastened to a hook on one of the metal bars extending upward from the platform.

Biff looked the equipment over, and gave the trapeze a hard tug to make sure it was bolted safely to its rope. Suddenly, the hook wrenched loose from the bar. The trapeze escaped from his grip and swayed out into space.

Losing his balance, Biff fell from the platform. With a scream, he plunged toward the ground far below!

14 Clown Rescue

His friends were horrified as Biff tumbled off the platform, and the spectators yelled in panic.

Out of the corner of his eye, Biff saw the trapeze swaying just above him. Frantically, he reached out, and a second later, he felt his hands strike against the bar! His fingers closed around it, and the next moment the trapeze carried him far out into space!

The spectators rose to their feet, shrieking. The sound echoed across the huge tent as Biff swung through the air over their heads. Reaching the end of the swing, he let go of the trapeze and landed on the opposite platform!

He gripped the scaffolding there to steady him-

136

self, then slowly climbed down, his knees still shaking from his frightening experience.

The boys from Bayport gasped in relief, but the spectators were in a frenzy of excitement.

They leaped to their feet, shouting that the circus was too dangerous and ought to be closed. There were screams for the police to stop the performers from going on.

MacIntyre hastened to the center ring and called for quiet, but his voice was drowned out by the audience. The crowd became increasingly unruly, and the ringmaster had to leave the arena after several minutes of attempting to restore order.

"They're getting out of hand," he said tensely to Tariski, who was standing near the entrance. "What are we going to do?"

"We might have to cancel the show," the director lamented.

Suddenly, a clown pushed past them and entered the arena. He had white and red greasepaint on his face, and broad black lines circling his eyes. He wore a battered top hat, an oversized vest, a coat with sleeves halfway to his elbows, and baggy pants. His shoes had turned-up toes, and he twirled a cane and carried a monkey on his shoulder.

The crowd quieted down a bit and began to watch as the clown strolled along, blowing a streamer at them. He leaned on his cane, which collapsed under him. With a yell, he fell to the ground and his top hat rolled away. The monkey retrieved it, leaped back on the clown's shoulder, and pushed the hat on his head.

The audience laughed and clapped their hands. Many sat down again as the clown collapsed his cane like a telescope and carried it under his arm. He walked on, continuing to blow his streamer. The monkey took his top hat and waved it, and the spectators cheered. Now almost everyone was sitting down to watch the rest of the performance.

While people's attention was focused on the clown and the monkey, Biff went out of the arena and joined his Bayport friends at the entrance. The clown ambled around the turn of the big top and came toward them along the other side.

After the boys had welcomed their lanky buddy and the excitement had died down somewhat, Frank pointed to the clown. "He's got an excellent act," he said admiringly.

"And he's sure getting a big hand," Phil observed.

"He deserves it," Tony declared. "He prevented a panic!"

"Good thing, too," said Biff. "I was afraid they'd start a riot when I climbed down from that platform, and I didn't want to have to risk my life a second time!"

The clown completed his stroll around the arena. The monkey skipped from his shoulder to the ground and bowed over the top hat. The clown bowed with him, then both went toward the exit hand in hand.

The spectators cheered and called for the show to go on, so MacIntyre hurried back to the center ring. In a booming voice, he introduced the tumblers and trained bears, the first acts in the two side rings.

Meanwhile, the clown stopped in front of the boys, who congratulated him on his performance. He cavorted about with a big grin, then asked in a low, guttural voice, "Where's Joe Hardy?"

The others looked around. They had not even been aware that Joe was not with them.

Frank scratched his head. "I don't know where he is—"

The clown pirouetted around him.

"I'm right here," Joe spoke up.

Frank and his friends turned in a circle without seeing Joe. "Where?" they demanded in unison.

The clown's grin became even broader as he pointed at himself. He was Joe!

"I was trying to figure out a way to stop the panic," he explained, "and I thought some comic relief would be best. So I ran to the clowns' dressing room, but they weren't there. That's when I decided to do the act myself. I put on the greasepaint and the costume, and took the monkey, which was in its cage. I had seen the routine rehearsed by one of the pros, or rather most of it. The rest I just improvised."

The two circus clowns came up, gaping at Joe, who apologized for using their props.

"Don't apologize, please!" one of them said. "We're glad you did. You made it possible for the show to go on, and you did a terrific job, too!"

"We watched you from the other end of the big top," the second clown declared. "You sure made a hit with the crowd."

Joe was a little embarrassed by the praise and moved off with them to remove his disguise and put his ordinary clothes back on.

Just then, the trapeze artists walked through the entrance. Biff explained to them about the loose hook.

"So that's why you did that death-defying leap!" said the female member of the group. "We're so glad that nothing happened to you."

"We'll take a new hook up to the platform and make sure it's properly bolted," her partner vowed. "We don't want to take the quickest route to the ground the way you almost did."

140

They thanked Biff for making the trapeze safe for them, then went to prepare for their act. Tariski stopped to chat with the boys for a moment and mentioned that he wanted to talk to the quick-thinking clown who had saved the show.

"Here he comes," Frank said and pointed to Joe, who had changed back into his clothes.

"Joe!" the director exclaimed. "That was a wonderful idea! And you were so good I'd be glad to hire you as a performer right now!"

Joe laughed. "I'm afraid I already have a job, even though we haven't made much progress. But Biff's accident was no accident. It was sabotage."

Biff nodded. "The bolt holding the hook in place had been unscrewed. Somebody must have climbed up there while all the rehearsals were going on."

Tariski's face turned pale, making the dark circles under his eyes more noticeable. "These incidents are getting more and more dangerous," he wailed. "You could have been killed!" Then he straightened up and his voice grew harsh again. "Boys, you must redouble your efforts to find the scoundrel who's responsible for this, or something terrible may happen!" With that, he walked away.

"That's easier said than done," Joe declared. "We don't even—"

He was interrupted by the prompter, who called, "Get the lion cage ready, please!"

141

"That's our job," Phil said to Biff and Tony, and the three moved over to a number of tall metal frames with bars extending from top to bottom. They piled the frames onto a motorized cart, which Tony, with Biff and Phil beside him, drove into the arena. His friends placed the frames on the ground in the form of a square, then Tony took a wrench and turned the bolts at the joints, locking the frames together.

When he was finished, the boys drove back to the entrance, where the lion tamer supervised them as they fastened the motorized cart to a file of cages holding the big cats. Tony moved back to the large cage in the arena, where he maneuvered each smaller cage into line with the door to the larger one. The lion tamer prodded his animals through the door, went inside, and closed the door behind him.

He had lions, tigers, and leopards in his act. Protecting himself with a small chair and cracking his whip, he made them jump through a hoop, run around in a circle, and leap up on their perches, where they snarled and roared.

Clawing at the legs of the chair, they bit at his whip. But they obeyed his commands, and the spectators applauded loudly as he bowed to them.

Frank nudged Joe. "It's fun to watch, but we have

a job to do. Let's see what's going on in the rest of the circus."

"I'll go with you," Chet offered. "I'm not on duty until after the big show's over."

The sideshow was dark when they got outside. They walked past the vacant stalls until they got to Arkin's. There they noticed a box labeled OCCULT COSTUMES.

"Let's have a look at that," Frank suggested.

They went in and squatted down around the box. Frank lifted the lid. The first thing they saw was a vampire costume. The rubber mask had two white fangs extending downward on both sides of the mouth.

"I wouldn't want to meet anyone in that getup in a graveyard on a dark night!" Chet declared with a shudder.

Frank lifted the vampire costume out and placed it beside the box. "How about this one?" he asked, holding up a wolfman mask twisted into a ferocious scowl.

Chet made a face, and Frank took out the next costume in the box. It was the zombie outfit.

"Nothing scary about that one," Chet said. "Just a uniform."

"That's because the mask is missing," Joe pointed out. "Arkin uses white greasepaint on his face."

Frank frowned. "I wonder whether the zombie at Hunter's Hollow uses paint or wears a mask," he said. "We've never been close enough to him to find out."

"I think it must be a mask," Joe said, "just because it's easier to take off than greasepaint. And our zombie must be able to change quickly. He couldn't afford to be caught with that glaring white face."

Frank held the Hessian uniform up and went through the pockets. "Empty," he said. "Not even a bullet for a Hessian musket. And the buttons look as if they've been on the coat since it was made. No, this isn't the coat we saw in the Hessian Hotel. But Arkin might have another zombie outfit hidden somewhere else."

He turned the neck of the coat and found a label reading: BARTON'S OF BURLINGTON.

"We'd better ask at Barton's about who's been buying Hessian uniforms lately," he said. He put the costumes back in the box and closed the lid, when suddenly they heard a noise behind them.

"Say, what are you doing?" a voice growled from the doorway!

15 The Lion's Den

The boys jumped to their feet and confronted Bones Arkin. He was holding a sword in his hand and waved it furiously as he stepped toward them. Warily, the young detectives moved apart, ready to defend themselves. But Arkin just lifted the lid of the costume box and tossed the sword inside.

"It goes with my Hessian uniform," he explained. "I was practicing with it out back when I heard you in here. Why are you so interested in my costumes?"

"We—uh—like your act," Chet spoke up. "So we thought you wouldn't mind us having a look at your outfits."

Arkin seemed pleased. "That's okay," he said. "Look all you want."

"We did," Frank told him. "Your disguises are really great. Enough to give an audience nightmares."

Arkin grinned at the compliment, and the three Bayporters waved to him as they walked out and continued along the darkened sideshow. They came to the circus vehicles and reached the van that had brought in the big cats.

"The cages are all under the big top," Chet said, his eyes lighting up. "That means the van's empty. You know something? I'm going to find out what it's like to be in the lion's den!"

Before the Hardys could comment, he pushed the bolt back and opened the door. Climbing in, he stepped forward across the straw floor. A lion tamer's wicker chair stood against the wall. Chet picked it up and hefted it.

"There's nothing to being a lion's tamer," he crowed. "I can handle this chair with one hand. All I need now is a lion!"

He was answered by a loud roar. From a dark corner at the opposite side of the van, a lion got to his feet and paced toward the boy, lashing his tail nervously. It roared again and again!

Chet gasped and turned pale. His eyes became as round as saucers. Mesmerized, his arm remained stiffly extended holding the chair in front of him. Seeing their friend's predicament, Frank and Joe climbed into the van. Frantically, they looked around for weapons with which to ward off the lion, but there was nothing to use except the chair Chet was holding.

"We can't do anything to help him," Frank hissed. "We have only our bare hands!"

"Maybe the little beastie won't want to take on all three of us," Joe said hopefully, but his voice sounded strangely strangled.

Just then, the big cat stopped in front of the chair. Snarling, it bit one leg. Then it lay down, placed its chin on its paws, closed its eyes, and went to sleep! The boys noticed it had a matted coat and a scraggly mane. The tuft at the top of its tail was nearly gone, too.

Joe started to chuckle. "It's an old lion!" he said. "I bet it can't perform anymore, so they left it here by itself."

"Let's not take any chances, anyway," Frank cautioned. "We'd better get out before it wakes up."

Chet recovered from his trance, even though his eyes were still bulging. He set the chair down carefully in front of the lion, then scrambled out of the van as fast as he could. The Hardys followed and Joe bolted the door shut again.

Chet brushed perspiration from his forehead with the back of his hand and let out a big sigh.

"Chet, I think your career as lion tamer has just ended," Joe said jokingly.

"Well, I stopped the beast with the chair, didn't I?" Chet challenged. "That's what a lion tamer does!"

Joe placed his hand on the bolt as if to draw it back. "Maybe you'd like to continue your performance, then?"

Chet moved off hastily. "Uh, no. Not today. I—I need a soda. My mouth is kind of dry."

The boys stopped for something to drink, then returned to the big top. Under Whip MacIntyre's direction, trained elephants were lumbering around one ring, and seals balanced basketballs on their noses in another. At last the show ended. After all the spectators had streamed out of the big top, the ringmaster snapped off the lights and departed for his van.

The Hardys held a final meeting with their Bayport friends. "We've come up against a blank wall," Frank grumbled. "Haven't picked up a single solid clue. Arkin seems to be on the level, we can't prove Reptilia let her snake out, all we know is that the saboteur is as active as ever."

"Look, why don't you return to Hunter's Hollow to see if anything's new there?" Biff suggested.

"We'll watch Arkin and keep an eye out for anything unusual."

Phil nodded. "Your cover won't last any longer," he added. "I mean, how long can reporters legitimately hang around?"

"I was thinking the same thing," Frank admitted.

"Why don't you give us Rolf's telephone number at the boardinghouse?" Tony suggested. "That way we can leave a message even if we can't get in touch with you."

"Good idea," Joe said and wrote the number on a piece of paper, then handed it to Tony. "I hope someone comes up with a lead soon," he added wistfully.

The following morning, the Hardys drove to Barton's of Burlington. It turned out to be a clothing store that specialized in making costumes for drama groups and other performers.

When Frank inquired about the Hessian outfit, the clerk consulted his ledger. "We've made only one of those," he declared. "It was ordered by a Mr. Arkin of the Big Top Circus."

"That doesn't tell us much," Joe said as they emerged from the store.

"It means either Arkin is the only 'ghost' in this area, or that the Hunter's Hollow zombie bought his getup somewhere else."

"Why don't we get the phone book and call other

costume stores in the county?" Joe suggested.

"Good idea."

The boys stopped at a public phone booth and consulted the directory. There were only two more shops that specialized in costumes, and they had not sold a Hessian uniform to anyone in years.

"Another dead end," Joe grumbled. "What'll we do next?"

"Let's talk to Rolf."

But when the Hardys arrived at the boarding-house, neither Rolf nor Lonnie was there. Frank called the acting studio, but the boys were not in rehearsal, either.

"There's no use waiting for them to turn up," Frank noted. "Let's go back to Hunter's Hollow. Maybe something has happened there since we left the Allen house."

They drove from Burlington and turned onto the road leading past Noah Williamson's farm. They met Williamson and his wife as he was driving out of the entrance. The two cars stopped nearly bumper to bumper, and the Hardys got out and walked over.

The farmer was very friendly this time, and sheepishly apologized for holding them captive in his house.

"We didn't realize an impostor had told us to grab you until the police confirmed it," he admitted.

151

"Oh, that's okay," Frank said. "Don't worry about it."

Neither mentioned the disabled car. Instead, Mrs. Williamson leaned out of the window and inquired, "Where are you boys going this time?"

"Back to the Allen house," Joe replied. "We're still trying to find the person who's responsible for the forest fires—"

"Don't!" she interrupted him. "We just passed the house, and we saw the zombie!"

16 The Game Is Up!

The Hardys were excited by the news. "Did he see you?" Frank asked eagerly.

"No. But he's lurking out there in the woods. Don't go, or he might do terrible things to you!"

"But we have to go," Joe told her. "Don't worry, we'll be careful."

"Remember, there's no protection against the supernatural!" she called back as her husband drove on. "You can't escape the zombie!"

Her warning made the Hardys shiver in spite of their disbelief in zombies.

Frank started the car and they continued along the road. Near the Allen house, Joe noticed a furtive movement in the woods.

"Hold it, Frank!" he urged. "Somebody's there. And he's taking care not to be seen."

Frank parked behind a grove of trees. Then he and Joe slipped through the grove to a bend in the road where they crossed over and moved toward the Allen house, using trees and bushes to shield themselves. They saw a flash of blue and red in the distance.

"That's the Hessian uniform!" said Frank in a low tone. "He's sneaking toward that clearing over there."

The Hardys followed, slinking from one cover to another. They hit the dirt behind a rhododendron bush when the figure peered back over its shoulder. Parting the branches, they saw the glaring, white, expressionless face.

"I hope he doesn't suspect we're here," Joe muttered. "What's he doing?"

"Beats me," Frank said in an undertone.

The zombie knelt down in a patch of underbrush and took something out of his pocket. Then a match flared up. A moment later, flames crackled in the dry wood.

"He's starting a fire!" Joe hissed, as the arsonist got up and ran through the woods.

The Hardys dashed forward. They began stamping out the fire just as the flames were starting to gather speed through the underbrush. It took the boys a few minutes to make sure they had extinguished the blaze, and nothing but a few square yards of burned vegetation remained.

"Where'd that creep go?" Joe asked grimly as he straightened up.

"I think he headed for the house. Let's see if we can catch him."

The young detectives sneaked through the woods to the front yard. Hitting the ground, they crawled across the open space to the end of the porch. Then they climbed over the railing, ducked low under a window, and reached the door. Joe pushed gently with his fingertips, and it swung open. But there was no sound inside!

After waiting a few moments, Frank slipped into the front room. Seeing it was empty, he motioned for Joe to follow him, and they tiptoed into the kitchen. The cellar door was slightly ajar!

Frank used hand signals to tell his brother he thought the zombie was in the basement. Joe nodded and they descended the stairs into the darkness below. There was no sign of a light, and no sound in the cellar. Joe tugged Frank's sleeve in the direction of the crypt. They were so familiar with the layout by now that they were able to make their way through the pitch blackness to the movable part of the wall. Feeling for the cinder blocks with his hand, Joe discovered that the passage to the crypt was open. No one seemed to be inside, so the boys went in.

Frank snapped on his detective's pencil flashlight. Shielding the beam with his hand as much as possible to avoid giving himself away, he played it around the crypt. Everything was as it had been before. Carefully, they stepped over to the stone coffin. Joe lifted the lid and Frank aimed his flashlight into the interior. Then the boys gasped!

Rolf Allen was lying inside the coffin, unconscious!

"He's probably been drugged," Frank finally ventured. "Let's get him out, Joe!"

Quickly, they lifted the lid and placed it on the floor next to the coffin. They were about to move Rolf, when suddenly a light gleamed in the cellar!

At once, Frank turned off his flashlight. He and Joe flattened themselves against the wall.

The light in the cellar became brighter as it approached, and the sound of footsteps drew nearer. A figure carrying a candle came through the door, wearing a Hessian uniform and a white mask!

"So that's the zombie face!" Frank thought.

Holding up his candle, the figure suddenly noticed that the lid was off the coffin. He swung around and jumped toward the secret passage, but the Hardys tackled him in midair. With a thud, the three fell to the floor. The candle went out, and a wild scuffle began, but soon the young detectives had subdued their adversary.

Joe held him pinned down, while Frank turned on his flashlight again, put his fingers under the chin of the mask, and pulled it over their captive's head.

The zombie was Lonnie Mindo!

17 Explanations

Frank took his T-shirt and bound Lonnie's wrists together temporarily, so Joe would have no trouble holding him while the older Hardy went into the kitchen to get twine. Then he searched Lonnie's pockets. Finding a matchbox, he lit the candle that had fallen to the floor during the fight. The box was marked with the words HESSIAN HOTEL.

"Just like the one you dropped at the first forest fire, Lonnie," Frank said.

"What are you talking about?" the boy snarled.

"The zombie's warning," Joe scoffed. "Come on, Lonnie, you're headed for the slammer!"

Forcing Lonnie to sit down in a corner, the Hardys lifted Rolf out of the coffin. They shook him and slapped his face until he came around. Then they took him and Lonnie upstairs, where Rolf sat down in a chair until his head cleared.

"Can you tell us what happened?" Frank asked him. "Do you feel all right?"

Rolf nodded slowly. "A little woozy, but otherwise okay. Except I can't believe—" His voice trailed off as he looked sadly at Lonnie.

"Rolf, how long have you known Lonnie?" Joe asked.

"I met him through an actors' workshop a few months ago. Since he was hard up for money, I invited him to stay with us. We got along fine and just recently signed up for the summer course in Burlington together. I really thought we were friends—"

Rolf's mouth hardened. "He fooled me all the time! He said that we should come here and investigate because the Hardys would never solve the mystery. He made a strange remark about the Hessian Hotel, and when I pressed him on it, he thought I had become suspicious of him." Rolf paused and sighed. "I really hadn't, but when we came down into the crypt, he put a rag soaked with chloroform over my face. That's all I can remember."

"And then he went off to set another fire," Joe said. "Luckily, we were able to put it out in time."

At this point, Lonnie realized that he did not

stand a chance, and he hung his head. Frank noticed the change in the boy's expression and took advantage of it.

"How did you know about the crypt, Lonnie?" he demanded.

"I discovered it accidentally," Lonnie replied. "Inside, I found some old documents. According to those papers, the Carltons built the crypt as the family tomb. The last Carlton put in the coffin for himself, but he sailed from New Bedford on a whaler that went down in the Pacific and was never seen again. I found that out from an old newspaper in the Burlington library while I was pretending to do research on Shakespeare."

"So none of the later owners knew about the crypt," Rolf inferred. "I'm sure my parents never heard about it when they bought the house."

"It was a perfect setup for Lonnie." Frank reconstructed the crime. "Obviously, he belongs to a gang of crooks. The ringleader is the one we call Squeaky Voice. He told him to set the fires. Who is he, Lonnie?"

"I'm not saying!" the youth cried out. "He'll get me out of this. Wait and see!"

"Well," Frank continued, "Lonnie dreamed up the Hessian zombie act. He knew the legend and he could get away with it because he's an actor. Also, he's been rehearsing *Julius Caesar* at the studio in

160

the afternoon. Since he plays Caesar, who's assassinated in the third act, he could leave long before the play was over."

"He could easily get out here and back to Burlington for rehearsal the following afternoon." Joe took up Frank's thought. "And he knew Rolf wouldn't be looking for him at the boardinghouse in the morning, because Rolf had morning rehearsals."

Rolf shook his head as if to say he could not comprehend how his friend had deceived him.

Joe continued the analysis of the crime. "The crypt gave Lonnie a safe hiding place for his Hessian uniform. He kept it in the stone coffin, where he could find it whenever he came to the house. He wore it so he wouldn't be recognized and to scare local people who might spot him, like the Williamsons."

"That's right," Frank said. "You see, Rolf, he only pretended to find the button from the uniform at the first forest fire, trying to scare you away from the house."

"Instead, I got you fellows to investigate," Rolf said. "Naturally, he didn't want that. I can see now, he was afraid you and your brother would solve the case."

Joe nodded. "That's why he tailed you to Bayport, to prevent you from meeting us. He stole Noah Williamson's car so there wouldn't be any dents on

161

his own. When we chased him away after he knocked you into the ditch, he doubled back to our house and saw through the window that you were talking to us."

"Exactly," Frank said. "Then he scooted back to Vermont ahead of us and left his uniform at the Hessian Hotel, which was used by his gang to store hot goods after their robberies."

"What a scheme!" Joe declared. "He was responsible for the zombie warnings, and the attempts to lock us in the crypt, and all the rest of it."

"He sure was," Frank said. "The gang took the uniform along with the hot goods from the Hessian Hotel after we escaped from them. Rolf, I bet Lonnie's been hiding the outfit under your nose in the boardinghouse from then on."

Lonnie's guilty look told the three boys that Frank and Joe were right.

"Well, we finally caught up with the zombie," the older Hardy went on. "And we also know some of the gang members. There's Pollard and Grimm to start with. Also Burrows, who only pretended to be a hermit. Lonnie sent us on a wild-goose chase to talk to Burrows so we'd be out of the way while he started the next forest fire. It must have scared him when it got out of control and nearly burned down the house. I bet the ringleader wouldn't have liked that. He probably wants the house, not a pile of ashes."

Lonnie became enraged. "I saved the house!" he yelled. "I stayed there to watch the fire. When the wind shifted, I phoned the state police and the fire department!"

Rolf looked at him soberly. "You also called me at the studio, pretending you were at the boarding-house, and told me you were leaving at once to help fight the fire."

Lonnie shrugged. "I hid in the woods, and when the police came, I told them I was a volunteer."

"And afterward you tried to lock all of us in the crypt," Frank accused him. "Lucky I kicked that cinder block into the opening in the wall before you pushed the control mechanism."

"Let's take a ride to police headquarters and turn him in," Joe suggested.

The four got to their feet. They were about to move to the front door when the phone rang. Frank picked it up.

A squeaky voice commanded: "Be at the Hessian Hotel in one hour! My courier will be waiting for you in the ballroom!"

18 The Unknown Courier

An inspiration suddenly hit Frank. Imitating Lonnie's voice, he said, "I'll be there."

Then the phone went dead. Frank reported the conversation to the others.

"That was Squeaky Voice, the ringleader of Lonnie's gang," he said. "He thinks Lonnie answered the phone and he wants him to be at the Hessian Hotel in an hour."

Joe grinned. "Too bad. Lonnie's going to be in jail instead."

"Right. Let's go." The Hardys took Lonnie to police headquarters, with Rolf showing them the way. Joe explained to the sergeant on duty that

Lonnie had started the forest fires, while Lonnie just stood and glared.

"He burned up part of our woods!" Rolf complained. "I'm pressing charges against him."

The sergeant took down the information and Lonnie was led away.

"Officer, the gang's still using the Hessian Hotel," Frank said. "You can probably catch the leader if you send a squad car there now."

The sergeant shook his head. "We've checked the place already and found it clean."

"That's because the gang got away before you arrived," Frank said. "How about trying again?"

"Sorry, but I can't spare the manpower for another wild-goose chase. I suggest you boys forget the Hessian Hotel and go home."

"But somebody called—" Joe began to argue, but he was interrupted by his brother.

"Come on," Frank said, and the boys went outside.

"We're not going to quit now," Frank said. "We'll just keep Lonnie's appointment ourselves!"

"How can we do that?" Rolf asked doubtfully.

"We managed to get into the place once before. I think we can do it again."

When they arrived at the hotel, the boys hid the car in a clearing down the road. Then they circled behind the trees to a place from which they could see the front door. There was no sign of life, and no cars were in the parking lot. The building appeared empty.

"There's no one here," Rolf whispered.

"Maybe there is," Joe replied. "The gang uses the back door."

"We'll use it, too," Frank declared. "If the courier is alone in the ballroom, we might be able to cut him off."

Quickly, the boys formed a plan. They sneaked around the building and approached the back door where Grimm had let the Hardys in. Frank pulled Rolf against the wall beside him, while Joe gently rapped the gang signal on the board across the door. Nothing happened. He took hold of the handle, cautiously eased the door open, and peered through the crack between the hinges.

"No one in the corridor," he whispered to his companions. "Let's go inside!"

Frank led the way in, followed by Rolf and Joe. They stopped at the stairs and listened for sounds of anyone on the upper floors. Hearing no footsteps there, they continued along the corridor to the room where they had seen the gang waiting for the message from the ringleader. Frank poked his head around the edge of the doorway. Seeing no one, he signaled to his companions to follow him toward the ballroom.

The door was open, and they saw a man sitting in a chair tilted against one wall. His hat was pushed back on his head, and his heels were braced on the chair rung. He was twiddling his thumbs impatiently, obviously waiting for Lonnie.

When he shifted his position to show more of his face, the Hardys gasped. *The man was Bones Arkin, the circus zombie!*

Just then, the sound of a heavy vehicle stopping at the rear of the Hessian Hotel could be heard. Quickly, the young detectives retreated into a room off the corridor, from where they could see into the ballroom.

The back door opened and footsteps advanced along the hallway. A man went into the ballroom. *Whip MacIntyre!*

Arkin turned around. "I thought you were Lonnie Mindo," he grumbled.

"Lonnie's on the way here," MacIntyre replied. "He got the message at the Allen house. The rest of the gang is in the bus outside. We're going to the new meeting place. Lucky the boss kept it vacant in case of an emergency."

"Do the Hardys know about it?" Arkin growled.

MacIntyre gave a sinister laugh. "Not a chance! The great detectives from Bayport haven't even been able to catch Lonnie," he added, with a note of sarcasm.

"But they found me eavesdropping on them at the circus," Arkin reminded him.

MacIntyre scowled. "That was stupid of you, Bones."

"Well, I convinced them I was tying my shoelaces when Frank Hardy jumped me. I'm sure they don't suspect me of causing those accidents. I just wish Biff Hooper had taken a nose dive from the trapeze after I loosened the hook! That would probably have shaken them all enough so they'd have gone back home!"

"You're right," MacIntyre grumbled. "And it would certainly have kept Joe Hardy from playing clown. With that little act, he prevented the panic that was about to break out—just what we needed to ruin the circus. Those pesty Hardys! If they give us any more trouble, we'll feed 'em to the big cats!"

The boys watched with bated breath, hoping that one of the crooks would mention the name of the gang leader.

As if in answer to the question in their minds, MacIntyre sighed. "And here we don't even know who the big boss is. He could be a member of the circus, or somebody completely different. But I guess it doesn't matter. His orders turned out to be right. He'll keep us on course."

The two men talked about the success of the robbery gang for a few moments, then MacIntyre looked at his watch. "I wonder why Lonnie isn't here yet?"

Arkin laughed. "He probably got hung up getting rid of that zombie outfit. He sure fooled the Hardys with that act of his. Don't worry about him. I'll wait till he gets here and then we'll follow you."

Rolf leaned toward the Hardys. "We have to stop them!" he urged.

Joe shook his head. "There's a busload of gang members out there. We can't tackle them all!"

"I'll go to the back door and see if I can get the license plate number," Frank proposed.

But before he could move, MacIntyre came out of the ballroom, strode down the corridor, and out the back door. Shortly afterward, the engine of the bus came to life. The vehicle could be heard moving toward the road, and the noise gradually died away.

Meanwhile, Arkin was still waiting for Lonnie in the ballroom.

Joe pulled Frank and Rolf near him. "Let's rush him," he suggested.

The three emerged stealthily from their hiding place. Frank and Joe positioned themselves at the ballroom door, but a floorboard creaked under Rolf's foot before he could join them. Arkin jumped up, saw the boys, and, with a curse, ran straight across the dance floor and over the platform where Frank and Joe had played in the country and western concert. Careening into the dressing room, he slammed the door and turned the key in the lock.

The boys ran after him. They threw themselves against the door but to no avail. To their chagrin, they heard Arkin raise the window, and realized he was climbing out. They rushed back across the ballroom, along the corridor, and out the back door. Just then, they heard the sound of a car gathering speed on the road.

"He got away!" Joe cried in disgust.

19 *Elephant Chase*

"He's headed for the gang's secret meeting place," Frank inferred. "But where is that?"

"Who knows?" Joe shrugged. "We can't ask him, that's for sure. We'll never catch him now. But since MacIntyre and Arkin are mixed up in the sabotage of the circus, it's possible that Tariski is their leader."

"You're right!" Frank exclaimed. "Let's go to the circus and check up on him. If he's the brains of the gang, we might trick him into giving himself away if we tell him we know about Bones and MacIntyre."

"What I can't understand is why these people want to destroy the circus," Rolf spoke up.

Joe nodded. "It doesn't make sense to me, either."

171

When the boys reached the circus, they met with Chet, Biff, Phil, and Tony. The four boys were surprised to learn that Lonnie Mindo was the zombie who had started the forest fires near Rolf's house.

"And you probably won't see MacIntyre and Arkin again," Frank observed. "Where's Tariski? He may be the gang's leader."

"We don't know where he is," Biff said. "We've been working hard getting ready for the next show."

"Well, at least we don't have to worry about sabotage anymore!" Chet exclaimed. "Frank and Joe solved that mystery. I would have solved it myself," he added with a grin, "except I was too busy."

"Practicing your act as the lion tamer?" Frank teased.

"I don't get paid for that," Chet said with a shrug. "If I did, I might have pursued it. Which reminds me, we'd better get back to work!"

Biff, Tony, and Phil agreed and returned to their jobs. Phil placed a roll of tickets on the counter at the ticket booth, while Chet opened his concession stand and prepared the grill for hot dogs and hamburgers. Biff checked the props for the acts on the trapeze and the high wire, and Tony worked on the motorized cart that brought the big cats in.

"I have to get back to the studio," Rolf said,

checking his watch. "Unless you need me here—?"

"Oh, no, go ahead," Frank told their friend. "We'll handle this."

"Okay, let me know what happens." Saying good-bye to the Hardys, Rolf went to the main road and caught a bus for Burlington.

Frank and Joe walked back along the circus caravan, and stopped at Tariski's van. Finding the door locked, they circled around the vehicle, peering through the windows.

"He's gone," Joe commented. "He must have cleared out in a hurry."

Frank nodded. "Arkin could have phoned him a warning that we're on to the gang. I guess Tariski's gone to the secret hiding place, too."

They checked the other vehicles, but nobody knew where the circus director was.

When they came to Reptilia's van, Frank chuck-led and said, "I'm half afraid to knock on the door. A boa constrictor might answer!"

"I hope it's friendlier than the last one we met!" Joe laughed and knocked.

"Who's there?" the woman's voice demanded from inside.

"Frank and Joe Hardy," Frank replied. "We'd like to talk to you."

The snake charmer opened the door, her pet boa draped over her shoulder.

"Come on in," she invited. "I have news for you."

The boys did and sat down on the sofa. The glass box holding the vicious reptile nearly touched their knees. The big snake hissed savagely, arched its back, and struck against the glass in an effort to get at them. Reptilia pointed to it.

"I caught Bones Arkin trying to get it out of its cage," she informed the Hardys. "I'm sure he was trying to disrupt my act. He must be the one who took the snake and put it in the equipment van when you boys were there that night!"

"That figures," Joe commented. "We know now that Arkin's been sabotaging the circus."

"And MacIntyre is in with him," Frank added. "That night, he saw us in the equipment van. He must have told Arkin to sic the snake on us."

Reptilia gave them a sly look. "Then I know the guy who's responsible."

"Who?" Frank and Joe exploded with one voice.

"John Tariski! I saw him and MacIntyre leave the circus together not long ago!"

"Have you any idea where they went?" Frank inquired.

She shook her head. "No. That's all I can tell you."

"Well, thanks anyway. You've been very helpful," Frank said, then he and Joe continued their tour of the caravan until they came to the office van. A man was running from the front door, carrying a case labeled TICKET RECEIPTS!

"It's Bones Arkin!" Frank exploded. "He's stealing the circus money!"

As the young detectives rushed forward, Arkin leaped into the van holding Leah the elephant. He started the engine and the van careened through the grounds. Circling the big top, Arkin reached the road and roared away.

"Come on, we've got to follow him!" Frank panted and rushed to their car. He squeezed behind the wheel and seconds later the Hardys were chasing the fugitive.

Their lighter vehicle quickly narrowed the gap between them and the van as Leah trumpeted at the pursuers. Her screech echoed over the countryside.

"I have an idea," Joe said suddenly. "I remember a bend in the road up ahead. Maybe we can cut him off there."

"Good thinking," Frank said. Soon they came to the wide curve Joe had in mind. Arkin followed the road, but Frank swerved into an open field and bounced across it to the other end of the curve. Then, halting in a cloud of dust, he let the car stand as a roadblock. Quickly, he and Joe got out.

The elephant van came around the bend seconds later. When Arkin saw the obstruction, he hit the

brakes to avoid crashing into the Hardys' car. With a loud screech, the van came to a stop a few feet away from it. Arkin slumped over the wheel with a tense sigh, while the elephant trumpeted wildly.

Frank wrenched open the door to the driver's side.

"Arkin," he said, "the game is up!"

20 Who Is the Boss?

Almost simultaneously, Joe grabbed the bag of money from the seat beside Arkin. "You outsmarted yourself," he told the crook. "We thought you'd never come back to the circus. But you were so greedy that you had to steal the money."

"We know about you and MacIntyre," Frank accused the man. "But where does Tariski fit in? And where's the gang's secret meeting place?"

Arkin glowered at the boys and refused to talk. They quickly bound his hands with his belt, then Frank drove the van back to the circus while his brother followed in the car.

When they arrived at the Big Top, Joe phoned

the police, who came and took Bones Arkin off to jail.

"Well, we caught one crook," Joe remarked. "But MacIntyre and Tariski got away. Who knows where they are?"

Suddenly Frank slapped his forehead. "Joe! MacIntyre said the secret meeting place is vacant. Maybe it's that empty office in Burlington! Remember—room 415?"

"I sure do! Perhaps the superintendent is a member of the gang. That's why he wasn't too friendly to us!"

The Hardys quickly drove to Burlington. They parked around the block from the office building, cut through a back alley, and reached the fire escape. Silently, they climbed up to the fourth floor, and crouched under the open window of room 415. Then they gingerly rose high enough to peer into the room.

Sure enough, the gang was gathered there— MacIntyre; Pollard, the concert director from the Hessian Hotel; Grimm, the doorman; Burrows, the phony hermit; and the superintendent. And— to the boys' complete surprise—there was John Tariski sitting in a chair with his arms and legs tied!

The phone rang, causing the young detectives to

duck again, since it was in the corner near the window.

The superintendent lied when he told us the phone was disconnected, Joe thought.

MacIntyre walked over and lifted the receiver, while the rest of the gang clustered around him. After identifying himself, he held the instrument so the others could listen in. The Hardys were close enough to hear as well.

A squeaky voice said, "Gather in the outer office. I'll be right over. We're moving out."

Then there was a click and the line went dead. MacIntyre placed the phone on the floor again and the men moved to the outer office. Grimm untied Tariski's legs and pushed him along. The circus director looked frightened and exhausted.

"Mac, what are you going to do?" he asked weakly.

The ringmaster grinned evilly. "That depends on the boss."

"Who's he?"

"I don't know. We just do what he tells us."

When they had all disappeared into the outer office, the Hardys could only hear a faint murmur of voices, and they could see nothing since the door was almost shut.

"Maybe we can push the window up farther," Joe suggested. "It's a chance to get in."

He and Frank placed their hands under the wooden frame and gently pushed upward. The window moved easily all the way to the top.

Silently, Joe led the way over the sill. Moments later, the brothers tiptoed across the office and peered through the crack in the door. Just then, footsteps approached along the hallway outside. The door opened, and Tyrell Tyson came in!

MacIntyre gaped. "So you're the boss!"

Tyson grinned. Pinching the bridge of his nose with his thumb and index finger, he intoned in a squeaky voice, "You bet I'm the boss! I planned all your operations at the Allen house and the circus!"

"You've been sabotaging my company!" Tariski accused him. "You put MacIntyre and Arkin up to it. Why?"

Tyson dropped his hand and spoke in his normal voice. "Revenge, John, revenge. We were partners, remember? Then you forced me to sell out to you. I never forgave you for that."

"But you were making the circus bankrupt with your crazy schemes!" Tariski retorted. "And I paid you a good price!" He shook his head in disbelief. "What are you going to do now?"

Tyson laughed brutally. "Finish off, that's what! That's why I had Mac fool you into coming here tonight. We're going for a sail on Lake Champlain, and toss you over the side of the boat. You'll sink to the bottom and stay there."

"Where do we go after we dump him?" Burrows asked Tyson.

"The Allen house in Hunter's Hollow. Lonnie Mindo called earlier and told me he locked Rolf in the crypt. The forest fires didn't scare the kid, so it's curtains for him. His parents wouldn't sell, so I got Lonnie to set the forest fires. He's just started the last one. Between Rolf's disappearance and the fires, maybe his parents will sell me the house when they get back from Europe. If they won't, we'll lock them in the crypt with Rolf. I have my heart set on that place. And it's just secluded enough to be our new headquarters."

"Why can't we keep using the Hessian Hotel?" Pollard inquired. "It's been a great hideout."

"When I was down at the courthouse the other day, I learned that the hotel is about to be taken over by the state. The authorities will tear it down to make room for a new highway," Tyson replied.

He sighed and added, "Besides, I *want* the Allen house. I've always liked it. It's—it's a personal thing."

"So we stash our goods in the Allen house until they come back from Europe?" Grimm asked.

"You got it. That is, after we get rid of the Hardys by setting a trap for them at the house."

Frank pulled Joe away from the door. "We have to nail these crooks!" he urged. "You stand watch while I call the police."

Joe nodded and Frank tiptoed to the telephone. He dialed the Burlington police station, and in a low voice explained the situation.

"We'll be right over," the officer on duty promised.

Frank hung up and then both boys climbed out of the window, in case the crooks tried to escape that way.

Suddenly, the wail of police sirens could be heard converging on the building, and squad cars jolted to a stop outside.

"It's the cops!" MacIntyre bellowed.

"Let's get out of here!" Pollard yelled.

The crooks made a dash for the door and piled out into the hallway, where they ran straight into the arms of the police! One by one, the criminals were handcuffed and escorted outside.

Tyson, however, had retreated into the back office and was racing to the window. He was about to climb out, when Frank shoved him roughly back inside.

"We thought someone would try this escape route," the young detective declared, "so we decided to block it." As Tyson regained his feet with a curse, Joe followed Frank through the window back into the room and the two youths quickly subdued the gang leader.

Tyson was too demoralized to resist further, and the boys delivered him to the police lieutenant, who had just untied the circus director in the outer office.

"He's the man who led the gang and arranged robberies all around Burlington," Frank told the lieutenant. "He also is responsible for the forest fires." Quickly, he explained the gang's scheme to occupy the Allen house.

"And he tried to sabotage my circus!" Tariski spoke up. "I'll press charges against him for that offense!"

The officer snapped handcuffs around Tyson's wrists. "We'll take all of them in," he declared. "Will you please come down to headquarters and make out reports?"

"We'll be glad to," Frank said.

Later that night, the Hardys phoned Rolf at the boardinghouse and told him about Tyson's arrest and the gang's activities.

"Wow!" Rolf exclaimed. "Did you ever make a catch! Boy, you're the greatest detectives ever. I'm so glad you came to help me!"

Frank chuckled. "Any time."

"Our play is on in a week," Rolf went on. "Will you stay and watch my debut?"

"I'm afraid we'll have to head home," Frank told him. "We have a few things scheduled ourselves."

"Oh." Rolf sounded disappointed.

"Maybe we can make it next time," Frank said. "Keep in touch and let us know how things are going."

"I sure will," Rolf said.

The next morning, the Hardys drove to the circus and said good-bye to John Tariski and their friends, who were planning to stay with the circus for the rest of the summer.

As they headed south for Bayport, they settled back in their seats, silently wondering if they would ever get another mystery to solve. Neither boy expected to become involved in *The Voodoo Plot* almost instantly after their return home.

Joe stared out of the window, then sighed. "Well, that's it. The end of the trail."

"Correction. The end of the track," Frank said.

"What do you mean?"

Frank chuckled. "The track of the zombie!"

You are invited to join

THE OFFICIAL NANCY DREW ®/
HARDY BOYS ® FAN CLUB!

Be the first in your neighborhood to find out about the newest adventures of Nancy, Frank, and Joe in the **Nancy Drew** ®/ **Hardy Boys** ® **Mystery Reporter,** and to receive your official membership card. Just send your name, age, address, and zip code on a postcard *only* to:

The Official Nancy Drew ®/
Hardy Boys ® Fan Club
Wanderer Books
Simon & Schuster Building
1230 Avenue of the Americas
New York, New York 10020

THE HARDY BOYS SERIES
by Franklin W. Dixon

Night of the Werewolf (#59)
Mystery of the Samurai Sword (#60)
The Pentagon Spy (#61)
The Apeman's Secret (#62)
The Mummy Case (#63)
Mystery of Smugglers Cove (#64)
The Stone Idol (#65)
The Vanishing Thieves (#66)
The Outlaw's Silver (#67)
The Submarine Caper (#68)
The Four-Headed Dragon (#69)
The Infinity Clue (#70)
Track of the Zombie (#71)
The Voodoo Plot (#72)
The Billion Dollar Ransom (#73)
Tic-Tac-Terror (#74)

You will also enjoy

THE TOM SWIFT SERIES
by Victor Appleton

The City in the Stars (#1)
Terror on the Moons of Jupiter (#2)
The Alien Probe (#3)
The War in Outer Space (#4)
The Astral Fortress (#5)
The Rescue Mission (#6)
Ark Two (#7)